THE FIRE FACTORY

THE FIRE FACTORY

by

Harry Ahearn

QUINLAN PRESS
Boston

Copyright © 1988
by Harry Ahearn
All rights reserved,
including the right of reproduction
in whole or in part in any form.
Published by Quinlan Press
131 Beverly Street
Boston, MA 02114

Library of Congress
Catalog Card Number 87-43281
ISBN 1-55770-021-4

Printed in the United States of America, 1988

Respectfully dedicated to the memory of Fireman First Grade Lawrence Fitzpatrick, who lost his life in a Harlem rescue attempt prior to the publication of *The Fire Factory*, and to Fireman First Grade John Toomey, Ladder 123, who died in a Brooklyn tenement after the submission of this manuscript to Quinlan Press.

The author gratefully acknowledges the editorial assistance of his youngest son, Lt. William T. Ahearn, Ladder Company 131 NYFD.

Contents

The Firehouse	1
Jack McBride	6
Harry Alcock	11
Building Inspection	16
The Bookends	24
Harlem Spectacular	30
The Adversaries	38
Jim Gillian	46
Oscar	51
The Chef	61
Pudgy's Brainstorm	66
Bernie Schwartz	77
The One Liners	82
Visitors From Outer Space	92
The Rope	103
The Study Group	107
The Nine Alarmer	114
Fun and Games	126
Quiet Evening in Harlem	137
The Street Kid	144
Another Quiet Evening	150
The Party	158
Requiem for a Fire Company	169
Aftermath to a Tragedy	182
Epilogue	188

The Firehouse

The two-story brick firehouse is hardly distinctive in appearance. Brown in front, whitewashed on the sides and back, it seldom rates a second glance. Nor is its location at East 114th Street and Fifth Avenue of prime importance. It's just another part of New York City's Harlem ghetto.

Perhaps the sign immediately to the right of the office window on the second floor might serve as a source of enlightenment. Some two feet high and three feet wide, the sign informs those interested that this is "THE FIRE FACTORY," home of Engine 58 and Ladder 26. That the sign has been ordered down, removed, and subsequently replaced may be indicative of the character of the firefighters serving this particular community.

The heavy mechanically operated doors are open on this humid September morning enabling passersby to see the imposing bulk of the Mack Pumper and the sleek streamlined mass of the 100' Seagrave aerial. It's rather functional this Fire Factory, strictly business. This firehouse was erected during a time of fiscal crisis, and so provides little more than a mustering point for on duty personnel and a storage facility for emergency equipment.

Toward the front of the building to the right of the pumper is an enclosed glass-lined partition surrounding the housewatch area. This is the nerve center of the firehouse. Twenty-four hours a day, seven days a week, a fireman is assigned to this location. Fireman Roger Brennan holds down the post for the moment. Fireman Third Grade Roger Brennan, to give him his just due. Red headed and freckle faced, Roger has been described as the hairiest goddamned proby ever appointed in Engine 58—a designation readily accepted by Roger who cheerfully informs those interested, "They ain't no flies on me!"

This morning at 9 a.m. Roger had reported for duty with the balance of the working platoon. Roger and the rest of the crew will be relieved at 6:00 p.m. The personnel replacing the current group will work through the night until the following morning, an interval of time the enterprising Brennan figures to use for some serious debauchery.

The firemen of New York City operate on a platoon system averaging slightly more than forty hours per week. Into these forty hours will be crowded more fire duty, more inspection activity, more injuries and more deaths than in forty hours in any other city on the face of the earth.

There is a wall immediately to the rear of the housewatch area and on this wall are two plaques. There's nothing unusual about these memorials and most firehouses have them. One commemorates two former members of Ladder 26 killed in a building collapse. The second honors the memory of a member of Engine 58 slain while serving with the armed forces. Roger seldom looks at these plaques because he's superstitious by nature and refuses to press his luck.

On the north side of the building adjacent to the pumper, a hose tower runs from cellar to roof. Near the tower the department has provided a locked area where the members store their gear. There is a pay phone in this area and Larry Fitzmaurice is using it. Five-eight, two hundred and twenty pounds, he's a veritable bulldog of a man and is known throughout the battalion as the "Fire Hydrant." Larry is the father of seven, with an eighth on the way and he is concerned regarding his wife's condition: "You gotta talk to that doctor, honey. I never heard of a ten month pregnancy!"

In the rear of the building is the kitchen and John Silensa is preparing a salad for the afternoon meal. John is a swarthy individual of average size and is assigned to the Ladder Company as chauffeur for this platoon. Even though he is reputedly one of the finest cooks in the department, he's not protected from the remarks of those objecting to tuna fish salad. Comments concerning the serving of cat food have already been passed. Silensa's approach to the matter is calmly practical: "Them animals—what the fuck do they know about good food?"

Sitting to the rear of the room is all six-foot-five inches of Jim Gillian, and he clearly objects to meals laced with mayonnaise: "How many times do I have to tell you that I'm on a diet?"

The man with the white hat reading the sports section of *The Daily News* is Lieutenant Anderson. A stocky gray haired veteran assigned to Engine 58, the lieutenant has been around for some twenty-seven years. Most of them have been spent in the Harlem area.

The two perusing the scratch sheet and trying desperately to pick a winner in the fifth at Belmont are Harry Alcock and Tom Henderson. Alcock, a former police officer, has been a department member for eight years. He's a tall thin man assigned to Engine 58 and he suffers the constant outrage of ribald humor concerning his family name. His continuous threats to transfer out of this "goddamned jungle" over the matter are no longer taken seriously. Henderson, medium sized and ruddy faced, has been assigned to Ladder 26 for seventeen years.

Outside of the kitchen on the apparatus floor are four brass poles placed near the four corners of the building. They provide for rapid response from the upper reaches of the building. All of these poles have been polished. The man who shined the poles is Fireman First Grade Pudgy Dunn, and he is now busily engaged in polishing the brass on the hook and ladder. Since Pudgy is on the lieutenants' list and this polishing is a task normally relegated to a junior member, he is outraged. For an interminable length of time he has been informing Oscar Ratner, Motor Pump Operator of Engine 58, that the situation is close to scandalous.

Even though Oscar has informed him that he's lucky he hadn't had charges preferred against him, Pudgy is not impressed. Pudgy's arrived late for work three tours in a row and is being punished by his superior, Captain Cullen. "Am I to blame for traffic-fucking-conditions on the FDR Drive?" Pudgy splits his infinitives.

Immediately to the rear of the housewatch area is a staircase leading to a basement which contains three rooms. One holds the oil burner, another the storage tanks and the third the department records for both units.

The area is now in use by two members menacingly facing each other. Silently they circle one another, each seeking an advantage. Oddly neither wears shoes. The taller man, black, easily six-foot-three, weighing no more than 160 suddenly and viciously kicks in the shorter man's direction. The kick is expertly blocked. The smaller man retaliates with a smashing jab aimed at the black man's groin. The blow is parried and both men pause, breathe deeply and walk around the area flexing their muscles. The almost daily karate session of Willie Burrell and Bill Murray is taking place. Murray, assigned to the Engine, and Burrell to the Ladder Company are the best of friends.

Upstairs, at the rear of the second floor is a washroom containing sinks, a shower and toilet facilities for nonofficer members. To the wall of one of the urinals an enterprising soul has posted a caricature of the Ayatollah Khomeine complete with instructions: "In order to hit objective, bucks with short horns must stand close to the bowl!"

Alongside the washroom is a bunk room containing twenty neatly made beds. Directly in front of the bunk room is an area filled to capacity with fifty lockers. A bulletin board is hung on the wall opposite the entrance to the locker room. An official pronouncement informs all that the board is to be used for department business, and most of the items posted on the board fall into this category. Others do not. Tom Henderson has placed a notice demanding the return of a pair of argyle socks that have been removed from his locker. The socks pinned to Henderson's demand are not argyle, nor have they been washed in some time. It's doubtful the hole in the toe of one of the socks can be repaired. A lengthy, impassioned note by Pudgy Dunn suggesting the formation of a football team for the purpose of playing the police department has been tacked to the bottom of the board and there is room for the signatures of those interested. To date there are no signatures and only one comment reading: "Are you out of your fucking mind?" A further note indicates Burrell's dog has had pups. He is obviously interested in disposing of the litter.

On the same floor toward the front of the building are three offices. On the north is located the office of Engine 58, in the middle is the area assigned to Ladder 26 and to the south is a spare office occasionally used by visiting chief officers. The office of Ladder 26 is occupied by Captain Ray Cullen. The captain is a veteran of thirty-three years and sits at his desk typing one of the monthly reports. Cullen is not surprised that this report will list in excess of six hundred runs with the usual high incidence of working fires. He's been forwarding this type of statistic for many years. The injury report listing the broken bones, the burns, the number of men overcome by smoke narcosis is also no surprise to this Harlem veteran. It's part of being a member of the Fire Factory. This is their story.

Jack McBride

Personnel changes are the norm in any firehouse, and certainly the Fire Factory is no exception. People retire, transfer, die or are promoted. Since there must be replacements, it's only natural that a member of the probationary class be assigned to Harlem. As sure as the sun rises in the east and sets in the west there won't be volunteers, and so the rather sad tale of yet another proby begins.

As Jack McBride climbed the subway steps at East 116th Street and Lexington Avenue, he made up his mind. That old-time buddy of his father is as full of shit as a Christmas goose. For the two months that McBride had been assigned to the Probationary School there had been the almost daily promise of a Flatbush assignment, and now this, Engine 58 in the heart of Harlem.

As a tall man McBride wouldn't have minded being posted to Ladder 26. Seemingly his 6'4" frame cried for such an assignment. Tall guys belonged in ladder companies, or at least that's what he's been told. It's all very disappointing, almost depressing.

It's starting to get dark as he walks up the gently rising slope leading towards Park Avenue. He's entering a new world and it's an environment sufficiently alien to awaken visions of an Arabian Knight's Dream. He'll find out soon enough that the residents refer to the area as LaMarquetta. To the firefighter this is the Casba.

There are dozens of small shops dealing in the variety of products local residents demand. Racks of gaudily colored print dresses, hundreds of boxes of shoes, and piles of fruits and vegetables are on display. Each store seems to be transacting business on the sidewalk. Dozens of customers haggle loudly with store personnel. Compounding this strange environment are the literally hundreds of persons who push along the sidewalk creating a complete sense of disorder. McBride feels disoriented. He has the sensation he's been transported to an alien planet.

As the big guy continues west breathing in the sights, the sounds, the smells and pushing his way through the hordes of people, he wonders how he'll make out in this new job. He's unsure of how he'll handle the smoke, the heat and the totally foreign experiences. He hopes he gets off on the right foot and wonders about the type of guys he'll be working with.

He reaches the elevated tracks on Park Avenue and crosses with the green light. Overhead a New York Penn Central train roars by. Briefly he stares into the huge municipal market located under the elevated structure. It's crammed with shoppers. In the distance he can hear a fire siren and wonders if he's missed a worker. A police car races by and McBride crosses the street and heads towards East 115th Street.

He's in a new part of town and the area has changed drastically. He's out of the Casba now and into a whole new ball game. He's passing a bar. It's packed to overflowing and the noise of a juke box blares out a blues number. There's the sound of a well played sax, the wailing of a horn and the complaint of a gal that's lost her man.

The outside of the bar is lined with blacks. Their glares are sullen and McBride feels uneasy. He senses their hostility. He walks fast. He can smell trouble. He must get away from that bar.

He's deep in the block now and the stoops are crowded on this pleasant October evening. McBride hears snatches of conversation. "Man, dig that big honky motherfucker!" It may be the kindest remark he'll hear prior to his arrival at the firehouse.

This is McBride's first trip to this part of Harlem. It's virgin territory to the big guy and totally unreal to him. He notes the number of overflowing garbage cans in front of each location, the variety of smells and the dinginess of each entrance. He continues along the block, picking up his pace. He's not at all comfortable. If there are parking facilities, he'll take his car next trip. Hopefully, the beatup 1968 Chevy will be up to the trip.

He's reached Madison Avenue and stopped for a red light. The traffic is heavy and he hopes the light will change. He's so concerned with getting out of the area that he's momentarily unaware of the guy standing next to him. Shifty eyed and rat faced, this bird's got something to sell. "Y'all lookin' for a piece of ass, man! I got me one real special bitch for you at a cheap price, man!"

McBride crosses the street without answering. Dickering with a pimp is not his idea of the proper way to start a new career. The tenements here are even dingier and the odors more oppressive. McBride spots a rat scurrying through a pile of garbage and the sight nauseates him. There's a group surrounding a character standing on the top of one of the stoops. Boldly this guy is passing out glassine envelopes in exchange for cash. McBride is not amazed. As a member of today's generation he's well aware of the realities of the drug situation.

There are project buildings across the street and McBride spots a group of girls jumping rope. Their endless grace intrigues him. Half a block further he sees a chain of persons leaving a tenement. The building is an obvious numbers drop.

He moves on. An ambulance and a patrol car are double-parked in front of one of the tenements. Two cops and an attendant are assisting a muscular male into the vehicle. McBride can't remember when he's seen more blood. Someone's worked this dude over. He bleeds from the arms and the chest and his face is almost destroyed. An hysterical woman, screaming shrilly, tries to force her way into the ambulance. The pushing, shoving crowd mindlessly interferes with the police, making their task more difficult. The roars of the crowd are almost incoherent. One voice stands out. "He done got cut by Rudy!" McBride is willing to admit that Rudy is a bad-ass dude he wants no part of. He pushes through the crowd and heads towards Fifth Avenue

There's a gathering in front of one of the buildings; it consists of a motley collection of human derelicts. McBride will soon learn the meaning of the term "Single Room Occupancy." This is such a place. It's literally a gold mine for the owners. Human debris is unloaded here in an attempt to dump them someplace out of the midtown public view. They stand in the last rays of the day's sunshine keening low, meaningless sounds. One of the bolder ones attempts to put the arm on McBride. "Hey man, how about some small change?" The big guy shrugs off the derelict's grip and continues on towards Fifth Avenue. The very touch of the guy makes McBride's skin crawl. "Y'all a cheap honky motherfucker!" McBride keeps moving.

He's at the corner of Fifth and 115th Street and he pauses for orientation. There's a bar on the corner and four well stacked chicks are swinging their pocketbooks and switching their hips. Clearly these women regard McBride as a potential customer. "How about a little nooky, honey? Give you a real good time at cut rate prices! I really dig big men!"

As McBride heads towards 114th Street he's again accused of being a motherfucker. He's puzzled. For years he's avoided association with such verbiage. Now, within the space of fifteen minutes, he's had that garbage flung at him on three separate occasions. It's something to think about.

He stops at the orange and blue of a Housing Authority Police car and asks directions. The firehouse is straight ahead and so is the advice of the Housing cop. "They didn't do you any favors sending you to this fuckin' jungle. Get your ass out of here as soon as you can!"

McBride heads south and he can see the firehouse clearly in view. He walks ahead and now the firehouse doors are opening. He hears the wail of a siren. The pumper is moving out. On the back step three stocky individuals are pulling on their fire gear. The hook and ladder is edging forward and several of the men stand in the street waiting to mount the running board. They're on now and the huge device picks up speed heading north against the Fifth Avenue traffic.

McBride looks after the apparatus as it disappears in the distance. He wonders if one of the guys might have a car.

Would it be possible to get a lift to the subway in the morning? Clearly he's had enough verbal abuse to last him a month of Sundays.

The possibility of returning to his old occupation occurs to him. Why lay out a bundle of cash for uniforms if he's not going to like his job? It's something he'll have to think about. Definitely it will be something to think about.

Harry Alcock

While there are easy tours and tough tours of duty in any firehouse, it's unfortunate, and probably indicative of life's realities, that there are more busy sessions for the members assigned to the Fire Factory than elsewhere. In conjunction with this line of reasoning, is the safe assumption that busy firehouse or not, some members create their own problems. Harry Alcock is such a person. At mealtime he didn't have to go for seconds. Silensa the cook hadn't forced an extra helping of parmesan upon him; he'd helped himself. Alcock was the one who'd gorged, not Silensa. Nevertheless, now, at this moment he chooses to ignore his own greed and persists in cursing Silensa.

As the pumper of Engine 58 speeds south along Fifth Avenue, Harry Alcock is feeling none too well. Once again, John Silensa has persisted in the use of garlic. Alcock conveniently forgets the second helping he'd foisted on his own protesting stomach. "That goddamned Silensa and his Sicilian slop! From now on I'm out of the meals!"

Silently Alcock prays for a false alarm. He'll take anything but a working fire. His prayers will remain unanswered. As the apparatus turns left on East 111th Street, Alcock sees that two top floors of an old law tenement are fully involved. Flames gush from every window. Scantily clad tenants stream from ground level in panic. Glass from the upper floors comes tumbling down, dangerously close to the vacating occupants.

It's Harry's turn on the nozzle, and as he pulls on his mask he hopes he doesn't puke into the face piece of his air-pack.

"That son-of-a-bitch Silensa and his friggin' garlic!" Once again it fails to cross his mind that he'd loaded up on the chef's delicacies as a matter of choice.

When they enter the first floor hallway, Alcock can see that the entire upper area is a mass of flame. Harry is convinced that anyone still at that level will not be coming down alive. As he turns toward the hallway exit Alcock can see the aerial of Ladder 26 being raised. The fire is banking down floor by floor. If Captain Cullen and his crew don't affect ventilation shortly, the Engine Company will be driven out into the street. The possibility that the fire could extend to other buildings and its potential for a greater alarm cross Alcock's mind. It obviously concerns the lieutenant as well. "Where is that goddamned water?"

The water arrives and Harry directs the stream up the stairwell as he works his way up the stairs step by step. The higher they go, the more unbearable the heat. The back of Alcock's neck feels ready to blister.

Ladder 26 has reached the roof; Engine 58 is sure of that. Evidence in the form of glass from the skylight comes crashing down. It's not the best method of ventilation. Surely the textbooks call for lifting the entire device in one piece. Textbooks, however, never consider skylights rusted into place for periods in excess of eighty years. Neither do engine company members crawling down smoke filled hallways.

Chief McCarthy's on the scene and he's all business. "Lieutenant, get that line into the nearest apartment. I've got Engine 91 stretching in right behind you. We're going to hold this baby to an all hands job!" His enthusiasm is far from contagious. While the practice of holding down response obviously saves the city money, such economy comes right out of the hides of the operating crews.

Willie Burrell and Tom Henderson are on the scene and working on the apartment door with axe and claw tool. As they force entrance a blast of heat, smoke and fumes drive the men to their knees. It's a horror show and the dancing flames are enough to remind one of Dante's *Inferno*. Harry inches forward in an attempt to bend the hose line so as to enter the apartment. As bad as it was behind him, it's now almost unbearable in this location. He's sick and his stomach bothers him. He's also a pro and there's no way in hell he's going to give up possession of the line. This is his night on the pipe. Tomorrow it's someone else's baby. Now, here in this Harlem tenement, he performs or he perishes. It's that simple.

Brennan is backing him up and that makes Harry feel good. As hairy as that kid is around the firehouse, he's a natural born firefighter. Once the chips are down he's thoroughly dependable. The presence of Fitzmaurice and Murray is added incentive to keep on pushing. The bull-like strength of this pair more than compensates for the lack of an extra hand, so needed but slashed by asinine budget cuts.

He's finally made the bend and directs the nozzle discharge towards the ceiling. Momentarily he shoots the stream directly overhead, enabling the returning water to fall on the crew. While it's hot, it's still fluid and will act as a coolant.

The lieutenant's right behind them and urging them on. He's an amateur psychologist who never berates his crew and always has a word of encouragement. "C'mon, guys—one more step—just one more!" They're into another room and have several more to go. The heat is as intense as ever. Alcock hears a crash of glass. Murray is working on one of the apartment windows with his helmet.

Harry crawls forward another step, then pauses. There's an obstacle in his way. He tries to move around the obstruction, feeling blindly for a way out of his dilemma. "There's something in my way! I can't figure out what the hell it is!" The lieutenant, shoving his way forward past Alcock, shines his light directly on the encumbrance and calls out in horror. "It's a woman—a pregnant woman. Get her the hell out of here!"

As Anderson relieves Brennan in backing up Alcock, Fitzmaurice, Murray and the Third Grade Fireman struggle to the rear end with their horribly burned victim. The thought that he'd been trying to climb over and around a tragically burned woman appalls him.

Alcock and the lieutenant push into yet another room and drive the stream into a weaving inferno of flame. There's a sudden ringing from an alarm device indicating a shortage of air in one of the tanks. It's the lieutenant's and as the officer whips off his face piece, Harry realizes he's down to zero air himself. They crawl forward a few more agonizing feet and Alcock's tank is out of air. Now they both know suffering. The toxic fumes attack both men as they stick with this nasty job.

Alcock and Anderson shove forward a few more inches. The officer isn't offering any encouragement now. He's merely surviving. They push forward into the apartment's last room driving the stream into the remaining traces of flame. Alcock shuts down the nozzle, drops it to the floor and staggers towards one of the apartment windows. Using his helmet he shatters the remaining shreds of glass, leans into space and vomits endlessly.

He is so sick. Never has he felt worse. Silently he prays for release from his agony. There is a brief moment when he feels death would be preferable to his present condition, and then he remembers the lieutenant.

Pulling back from the window, Alcock staggers towards the reclining figure. Anderson, barely conscious, is on his hands and knees and peering through the smoke-filled atmosphere. His whisper is barely audible. "Are you okay, Harry?"

The thought that this beaten man's first concern would be for him affects Alcock visibly. He's close to tears. "I'm all right, lieutenant. I'm fine. Let's get the hell out of here!"

Assisting one another, they stagger through the battered apartment. Harry notices the broken windows, the battered furniture, the paint-blistered walls, the scattered remnants of some ghetto occupant's life.

The dishes, cups, saucers—strewn throughout the apartment—are all smashed. A child's teddy bear floats face downward in water several inches deep. Slowly they make their way from room to room and out into the hallway. The stairway is lined with hose. There's at least four lines stretched into different apartments. From up above they hear the pounding of an axe; someone is opening up and searching for avenues of fire travel.

A cascade of water flows down the stairway. They pass a

few of the operating crew and can hear the voices of those working overhead. Slowly they plod toward the exit. Alcock has a terrible headache. He keeps trying to remember what it was that had been bugging him all evening. Hadn't it been something about Silensa and his cooking? Wasn't there some decision he'd come to concerning the meals?

The harder he tries to concentrate, the more confused he becomes. Finally he puts the situation to rest. "Fuck it! I'll take care of it tomorrow. That's what I'll do. I'll take care of it tomorrow!"

Building Inspection

Some things never change and can never be avoided. Building inspection in Harlem is one of life's inevitabilities; any member assigned to the Fire Factory can tell you that. The firefighters assigned to these units can duck and wriggle and squirm, but sooner or later out of the door they go, involved in what these men regard as a total waste of time. The area of assignment matters a great deal. Inspecting a school, a church, or a library is AOK. Unfortunately, Harlem's schools and churches and libraries are in the minority. The tenements —the ever present tenements—are the stark reality.

There's an inspection scheduled for today and the mood of the men assigned to Engine 58 matches the weather. It's threatening to rain on this Tuesday morning in November, and the members assigned for duty are far from happy. It's not the rain that gets them down. What really gripes them is the certainty that at 9:30 the unit will be leaving for building inspection. Normally the men can take this department function or leave it. The district selected is what bothers them. East 117th Street between Madison and Fifth Avenue is hardly their idea of a picnic area.

Perhaps Oscar Ratner best expresses the opinion of the fire fighting personnel assigned to this unit—"I've been inspecting that friggin' pesthole for the last twenty-two years I've been here and they're still throwing garbage out of the windows."

The performance of apparatus field inspection duty in most areas is something to be tolerated. Here, in the Harlem ghetto the attitude is somewhat negative. "Like shoveling shit against the tide" is Fitzmaurice's somewhat inelegant opinion. Since the fruitless hours of inspectional activity result only in a constant increase in fire duty, Larry's attitude is sharedby his peers. "Show me some results. Just show me one area of progress!" is Lieutenant Anderson's plea. There is none.

It's ten minutes prior to the scheduled time for departure and the members prepare for the inevitable. Building inspection cards, summons books, violation order forms, pencils and the variety of paraphernalia necessary for the operation are secured on the apparatus.

True to form, Roger Brennan contemplates absenting himself from the program. Rapidly his mind races over the variety of ploys he's engaged in past attempts to avoid this unpleasantness. Should he claim an attack of the trots? Quickly he abandons that ruse. It had been used successfully several weeks ago and can't be used again. How about his old war injury? Good thought, but no cigar. Pushing that gimmick might result in medical leave and a possible assignment to light duty. Roger has no desire for a pencil pushing detail at headquarters. The thought of bucking the subway five days a week brings on a momentary attack of nausea.

Roger looks at the clock—three minutes to countdown. Things are looking desperate and it's time for drastic action. Would anyone in the ladder company be willing to switch tours? He abandons the thought because Battalion approval, absolutely essential, would never be forthcoming. Frantically he races to the pay phone in the locker room cursing himself for not thinking of his sister sooner. Sister Lillian is expecting a baby. Surely Lillian, eight months pregnant, would require her brother's emergency assistance.

Damning his clumsiness as he drops his quarter, Roger reaches for another coin. Hastily he dials the phone. Busy— the goddamned line is busy. Dames, you can never trust a dame. What the hell can an eight-months pregnant woman have to talk about at nine-thirty in the morning?

The apparatus is turning over and Lieutenant Anderson is staring at Roger. "Do you," asks the lieutenant, "require a special invitation?" Mounting the rear step of the apparatus

Roger glares moodily in Alcock's direction. "Fucked," he informs Alcock. "Fucked by the fickle finger of fate!" Harry is puzzled. "What the hell is this guy raving about?" Roger's further explanation concerning pregnant women being barred from the use of the phone prior to 9:30 a.m. is far from enlightening.

It still looks like rain as the apparatus heads south on Fifth Avenue. Since this isn't an emergency response, they'll have to go with the traffic. South on Fifth, east on 111th, and north on Madison will get them to their destination. If Lieutenant Anderson could think of a longer route to circumvent the inevitable, he'd give it a whirl.

They swing into 117th Street and into the area of activity. For the next three hours this will be their battleground. The block is lined by rows of eighty-five year old tenements. Each building is five stories in height and approximately 60x80 feet in area. If there had been a time when the surroundings were pleasant, that time has long since vanished. Every structure has at least six smelly, overflowing garbage cans near its entrance. Each building has a distinctive aroma. The odors of unwashed bedding, urine stained hallways, defective plumbing and greasy cooking aromas blend into a mixture more solid than gaseous. "Thick enough to be sliced" is the way Harry Alcock phrases it.

The street is crowded with parked cars and the apparatus is forced to double park. Even the hydrant spaces are occupied, and since Lieutenant Anderson is far from reluctant in regard to the issuance of tag summonses, such occupancy will be costly.

The presence of automobiles in an area of abject poverty has often puzzled these firefighters. How can a guy who can't afford a refrigerator handle an expensive gas guzzler? Nevertheless, there they are—all shapes, sizes and colors. Ranging from beat up heaps to a Lincoln Continental, they line both sides of the street.

There's little doubt concerning the ownership of the Continental. The sleek, flashy, less-than-a-month old model belongs to Motown Freddy. Freddy is one of the area's more opulent entrepreneurs and he deals exclusively in drugs. Coke, hash, speed, angel dust, heroin—name your pleasure and Freddy has the goods. He's the main man in this wholesale drug market and he's been here for a long, long time.

On this miserable morning four of Freddy's henchmen occupy a variety of spots along the block, and they are not without customers. A seemingly endless stream of humanity heads in the direction of the drug merchants. Fitzmaurice is amazed. "They're so goddamned well organized, each one of these bastards is handling a different kind of drug!" For no apparent reason he adds, "I hope they all wind up with a dose of the clap!"

It's 9:45 and time to begin this senseless charade. Three of the men are handed a violation order book and assigned a building for inspection. The lieutenant and Oscar will remain at street level. There's reason enough for Oscar's presence. He's the Motor Pump Operator and will monitor the radio. Lieutenant Anderson's sidewalk presence will be unofficial in nature since he is taking advantage of the prerogatives of rank. In his own words, "I'll take care no one steals the apparatus." He'll also avoid proximity with the variety of hell-holes lining this sordid street.

As Fitzmaurice approaches his inspectional area, he becomes aware that his building is the center of commercial activity. One of Motown Freddy's underlings is busily swapping small glassine envelopes for cash. His customers are well-hooked wretches. They slink up, snatch their envelopes and hustle down the block assuming what the area defines as the "I've got mine strut!"

Being a wiseguy, the pusher must make a comment. "How about some smack, man? Help you pass the time down at that firehouse 'stead a playin' all that pinochle!" "Shove it up your ass!" is all the reply Fitzie has to offer. He's been on this block before. Causing a commotion by decking this dealer in human misery will accomplish nothing. He takes a deep breath and walks into the tenement hallway.

For a moment Fitzmaurice has difficulty adjusting. The fetid, overpowering stench is nauseating and the ammonic odor of urine a sure indication that the halls have been used as a latrine. "A regular fucking five story urinal this joint," is

Fitzmaurice's rationalization. He heads for the hallway leading to the first floor landing.

High above an infant wails. Larry is appalled. What chance does that baby have? He reaches the first floor. He plans to climb to the roof and start his inspection by working his way down to the basement.

There's a brawl going on as he reaches the second floor. The shrieks of a woman physically involved with a man are ear-piercing. Larry considers knocking at the door and intervening but reconsiders and heads for the third floor. There's the sound of glass breaking. The loud, raucous, deep baritone voice of the male occupant sounds triumphant. "Bitch, don't never mess with my money again!" Larry wonders how tough this dude would be up against someone his own size and weight.

The light is out on the third floor. Larry will have to be careful. No sense in being mugged by some scoundrel enterprising enough to douse the hall light. Nevertheless, he is trapped. It's not a mugger that gets him, but his inability to see clearly. Some person, too lazy to use the accommodations so evident to most people, has defecated in the hallway. Fitzmaurice is outraged. "Just what I need—a footfull of shit!"

The fourth floor is sufficiently illuminated for Fitzie to note a huge pile of garbage lying outside one of the apartment doors. There's a rustling behind the debris and Larry has no intention of determining its cause. Cat or rat, let it rustle. He'll hand out a violation order if, and when, he locates the super.

There's a flow of water seeping under a fifth floor apartment door. Someone's toilet facilities have overflowed. Just another odor to combine with the endless variety of smells available in this social cesspool.

The landing leading to the roof is occupied by three junkies; sleeves rolled to the elbows, they're shooting up. One, on the nod, sits on the top step seeking whatever escape from reality that his habit avails him. The second prepares to inject himself. The third waits his turn. Not one pays the slightest attention to the inspecting fireman. He offers no threat and to them he's not even an intrusion.

As he brushes past these human derelicts, Fitzmaurice opens the bulkhead door and steps out on to the roof. The weather is even more threatening. That doesn't bother Fitzie. He's momentarily out of that horrible environment and he inhales deeply, filling his lungs with an atmosphere relatively free of the stench of urine, garbage and overflowing toilets.

Larry walks to the edge of the roof and gazes down to the huge pile of garbage littering the back yard. It's almost up to the first floor. The mound increases as one of the tenants tosses more refuse out of a window.

The stockily built Fitzmaurice looks up at the threatening sky. He hears the droning of a plane heading out of Kennedy and ponders its destination. He looks over the edge of the roof towards Madison Avenue. The traffic is heavy as it heads north on the one way street. Once this tour is over he'll be glad to be part of that traffic. He takes a final look around and heads towards the bulkhead door. He has a few violations to serve on the super.

The junkies are all on the nod. One stands leaning against the wall. Another lies stretched out on the floor. The third holds on to the banister. Larry shakes his head in sorrow. "Poor bastards. Poor, poor bastards."

There's a radio blaring as he heads towards the fifth floor. One of the tenants is musically inclined. As Fitzmaurice skirts the escaping flood of toilet overflow, he notes the appropriateness of the music. "It isn't raining rain you know. It's raining violets." Larry is convinced he is not tiptoeing through any violets.

As he descends from floor to floor, Fitzie makes mental note of the variety of violations. He'll include them all in one form to be issued to the super. He assumes he'll locate the individual in the basement and heads in that direction.

He's been in these Harlem basements before and the area offers no surprises. It's dimly lit and the aromas defy description. The foul smell of human defecation contrasts strongly with the odor of decay. Larry is certain that something died down here. A variety of trays bearing rat poisoning offers a clue. There's some dead rats here. There's also an abundance of the species still living. Their scurrying presence gives Larry the creeps. He'll get out of here as soon as possible. "Super!" he calls, "Super! Where the hell are you?"

There is no answer. The surrounding debris consisting of soiled dirty mattresses, broken furniture and old newspapers offers no clue to the super's whereabouts. "Super, get your ass out here!" Larry feels panic setting in. He decides to leave but hears a shuffling sound and turns.

It's obvious that the huge black man facing him had once been powerful. Now stumbling towards Fitzmaurice, wine bottle in hand and soddenly drunk, he's merely a pathetic shadow of a normal human being. "Y'all lookin' for me?"

Fitzmaurice hands the super the violation order and the huge man, swaying under the heavy load of alcohol, peers drunkenly at the form. "Hey, man! What I supposed to do with this?" Fitzie backs towards the cellar exit. "Give it to the landlord!"

The overall-covered giant is overcome by Fitzie's wit. Grasping his bottle in one hand and the violation order in the other he roars up a storm of laughter. "Hey, man, you a real comedian! The city owns this motherfuckin' building. The landlord done abandon it! Don't you firemen know anything? Who I give this thing to? The Mayor? It's Mayor Koch's baby now, man! Here, take it back and give it to him!"

The giant's laughter bounces from wall to wall stilling even the scurrying of the huge rat population. Larry feels that this is a nightmare. He's got to get out of here. Abandoning all pretense at dignity, he takes off and heads for the exit. He's got to get a breath of fresh air and reach some semblance of normality.

It's raining as he reaches the street and he starts towards the apparatus. Ratner is waving towards him. There's good news. The department brass have decreed that the weather is sufficiently inclement to order the dispatcher to recall the inspecting units.

It's really pouring now and still the weather makes no impression on these firefighters. They're free of this pesthole. They're free of the ammonic stench of urine, the scurrying of rats, the ceaseless sale of narcotics and the utter degradation heaped on the heads of the pathetic residents of this totally abandoned community. They're also escaping their own consciences. These same men who entered the block long of face are leaving singing, actually singing. As they mount the back step they're raucously in chorus: "It isn't raining rain you know. It's raining violets!"

As the apparatus pulls down the block towards Fifth Avenue, Motown Freddy activates the electric device controlling the window of the driver's side of the Continental. Looking out he can still hear the singing. He turns towards the dealers, all busily pushing his merchandise. Could any of his dealers have handed out a few samples to the firemen? There had to be some reason for all that celebrating.

"Still," he reasons, "one never knows! How the hell can anyone figure out a fireman? Anyone willing to fight fires in these tenements at the wages they get simply can't be figured out at all." He closes the window. "Sure as hell ain't no sense in using my heater to heat up the whole neighborhood. No sense at all!"

The Bookends

Every firehouse has a number of distinct personalities assigned to it. Firefighters come in all sizes, shapes and colors. That the personnel assigned to Engine 58 and Ladder 26 are rather bizarre is understandable. Where else would headquarters place the people on the payrolls of these units? The men assigned here were born to be Harlem firefighters. They'd be out of place elsewhere. They'd stand out like sore thumbs, anachronisms, screaming attention to themselves, and possible embarrassments to another community. Here they fit in, hardly noticed, a part of the neighborhood. They are assets worth their weight in gold as long as they remain north of 110th Street. Fitzmaurice and Murray are such a pair.

Since one of the primary rules of chemistry concerns the storage of violently reacting substances, there are those who see little sense in assigning Larry Fitzmaurice and Bill Murray to the same quarters. It would be truthful to say that not just a few of their peers feel that they should be separated by at least a borough.

Alone, their reactions are rather normal. They're both family men who assume and meet obligations in routine fashion. Together their reactions are kaleidoscopic in nature—rather like a Fourth of July celebration or the outbreak of World War II.

Individually, Fitzmaurice is referred to as "The Fire Hydrant"—a description aptly fitting his size and build. Murray is known as "The Mole"—a pseudonym requiring more elaboration. An ardent disciple of the martial arts, his continuous karate workouts in the firehouse basement have led to this rather unglamorous alias. Together, and they are seldom apart, they are referred to as "The Book Ends."

It's not that they look like twins—not that at all. Facially there's little resemblance. Fitzmaurice has a puckish countenance. He's rather elfin in appearance, sports a pug nose, and has what is often described as "the map of Ireland" for a face. There's no doubt that Murray's face is Irish, too. It's simply a different Irish face than Larry's.

Their respective builds are what identify this pair and earn them their collective nickname. Both are 5'8" and both are constructed along remarkably similar lines. Hitting the scale in the vicinity of 220 and without an ounce of fat between them, they're an awesome pair. Sitting together at the table in the firehouse kitchen, or occupying adjoining bar stools in any local pub, they're a spectacle that would inspire respect from any normal person. Unfortunately, the New York scene is not necessarily populated by normal people.

Their episodes with those seemingly bent along masochistic lines have become legend. Despite attempts to mind their own business, they have found it necessary to litter the outside—and sometimes the inside—of a variety of taverns with the bodies of those prone to tempt the fates.

It's not only body structure that identifies these clone-like characters, but their backgrounds as well. Both come from fire department families. Larry's father is a retired fireman and Bill's dad served nine years as a lieutenant in Engine 58. The fire department is not the only connection between these two; both possess an inordinate love of football. They've been starting members of an outstanding semi-professional club for the past eight years, an activity that has been the bane of their wive's existence. These women are considerably justified in feeling that exposure to Harlem fire duty is sufficiently hazardous without the added risk of pigskin mayhem.

Larry is the older of the two and has been a department member for some fifteen years. Bill's been around for five. While Fitzmaurice's appointment to Engine 58 was purely routine, Murray's took a bit of doing. He's a graduate of the United States Merchant Marine Academy and there were those in official fire department positions who regarded his appearance as an opportunity to buttress the forces of the Marine Division. Murray thought otherwise. He convinced his dad that an assignment to a busy unit was preferable to growing barnacles in a marine company, and this resulted in sufficient pressure to attain his wish. This maneuver was deeply regretted by the elder Murray on many a sleepless night.

Perhaps a harbinger of things to come was Murray's first St. Patrick's Day parade in the uniform of a New York City firefighter. Actually, he and Fitzmaurice missed one another and had marched up Fifth Avenue in separate sections of the fire brigade. Annually the Fire Fighters Holy Name Society throws a monumental wind-ding featuring huge quantities of hot dogs and beer. Since the refreshments are served at a local National Guard Armory, finding one another amidst the thousands of blue-coated individuals had been a problem.

Being persevering, they'd come together, and being rather restless, they'd left, heading south on Madison Avenue. As mentioned previously, there are those who feel that either of these two, on his own, should be left strictly alone. Together, there's a chemistry that requires the adventurous to try them out. They'd only gone three blocks when they'd chanced on a group of five construction workers obviously feeling no pain. It was evident that these characters were in a mood to celebrate boisterously. "Hey, look at the two faggots in fire department uniforms!"

While normally there might have been discussion of a sort, no one with a drop of Irish blood could take kindly to such conduct on St. Patrick's Day. And so Fitzmaurice delivered a smashing blow to one of the revelers driving him in front of an oncoming Madison Avenue bus. The bus was driven by a huge black man caring little for St. Patrick's day or its celebrants, and this may have saved the life of the construction worker. The bus was stopped on a dime, which did little for the horde of celebrants within the vehicle who were deposited in a variety of embarrassing positions towards the front of the bus.

Since Fitzmaurice and Murray were busily clobbering the hell out of the remaining four construction workers, they had little time to pay attention to the outraged demands of the driver. "You Irish motherfuckers—go home and sleep it off!"

The melee was short-lived. Actually it was no contest. Oddly enough Fitzmaurice was annoyed with Murray. "How many times do I have to tell you to shove that karate stuff up your ass? If you can't use Marquis of Queensbury rules against chumps like this, join the Girl Scouts!"

As adept as Murray is in the martial arts, his ability along those lines is insignificant when compared to Fitzie's strength as an arm wrestler. While certainly there are those few capable of handling Bill, the man having the ability to put Fitzmaurice's arm on the table hasn't been found. The strength of these two has caused Captain Cullen a constant problem. Members assigned to Ladder Companies are usually big men and men of stature are normally macho in nature. Some seventeen accident reports were filed before the captain laid down an order: "Any member of Ladder 26 arm wrestling with Fitzmaurice or engaging in karate workouts with Murray will have charges preferred against him." Gillian had been flung up against the basement wall on some half dozen occasions. Undaunted, he'd finally wound up with a dislocated shoulder after issuing a challenge in Fitzmaurice's direction. Because he was only one of six members of Ladder 26 similarly affected, the captain gave his ultimatum.

Like most football players, the Book Ends play a hard, tough game free of cheap shots. Again like most football players, they're quite capable of responding when challenged. Playing against a top-notch team from New Jersey, Murray had his bell rung by a particularly nasty individual. The guy leaped with joy as Bill was carried from the field. He didn't leap for long. Outraged that his friend had been cheap-shotted without even a penalty flag being thrown, Fitzmaurice had utilized the next play to even matters. He was ejected from the contest, but that had no meaning. He consoled himself with the thought that it took some ten minutes to pry the helmet from the cheap shot artist's head. The forearm he'd used had not only destroyed the protective device, it had removed its occupant from any connection with football for the balance of the day.

It would be inconsistent to assume that *all* of the misadventures befalling these two could be attributed to others. They're quite capable of fouling up on their own. Consider Murray's collection of antique guns. He possesses quite a few. A time came when the testing of one of these ancient devices seemed the only thing to do. Heading for a local tavern, the Book Ends messed around with a mixture of black powder while discussing at great lengths the appropriate quantity required for maximum effectiveness. Into this scene had wandered Rosie, an elderly female. Rosie's traditional visits to the tavern had pleased the owner. She'd enter, sit down at the nearest bar stool and gesture in the bartender's direction. Immediately she'd be supplied with a beer and a shot of rye. Normally, Rosie would settle for two of these combinations, throw her money on the bar and leave. Never in the memory of the oldest patron had this lady been heard to utter a single word. The Book Ends would be responsible for breaking this tradition. Turning to greet a friend as he lit a cigarette, Larry deposited the still lighted match in the mixture of black powder with stupendous results. The ensuing explosion was almost catastrophic in nature. Barroom habitues who hadn't moved rapidly in years were diving in all directions. All save Rosie. Steadily she regarded the dust of years as it settled from the ceiling into her drink and finally she uttered her first words: "*You assholes!*"

Many felt it was fortunate the incident had caused no injury other than the loss of Rosie's patronage. She'd regally removed her business to less hazardous environs. This, however, had not been the case. There was a frightful loss of pride and dignity on the part of Bernie Muldoon, combat veteran of World War II. In his own words he had shit himself from head to toe. It would be a long time before Bernie would speak to the Book Ends—a very long time.

Being rather persistent by nature, the Book Ends had merely postponed the actual firing of Murray's weapon. On yet another evening they'd wadded the gun with a load of wet toilet paper and fired the device with great precision. Unfortunately for Police Officer Harry Kramer, who'd just completed a four-to-twelve at the 63rd Precinct, he'd selected that very moment to emerge from his battered Mustang. "I thought fuckin' World War Three had started. I was removing wet toilet paper from my hair and ears for a week." Happily for the Book Ends Kramer is a long time friend and has a sense of humor.

Lieutenant Anderson also has a sense of humor. How else can one possibly explain his willingness to accept this "Odd Couple." Despite offers to split the pair by assigning them to groups as far apart as possible, he's quite content to have them working under his jurisdiction. "If we never had fires, I wouldn't care if I ever saw that pair of crazy bastards!"

His rationale is obvious. Harlem has an inordinate number of fires and the Book Ends are unparalleled in professional expertise. He's sure of one thing, however—definitely sure. "If I ever transfer to Whitestone, you can bet your ass I won't invite that pair to join me." The lieutenant is a practical man. Very practical.

Harlem Spectacular

Firefighting is the name of the game in Harlem. There's lots of it and it can't be avoided. Anyone concerned about an excess of such activity is assigned to the wrong area. Of course, there are those who flee the scene in short order and endlessly discuss their adventures when in safer climes. Others remain and have little to say concerning their experiences. The captain of Ladder 26 is such a person.

Nothing in this Harlem ghetto amazes Ray Cullen. For thirty-three years he's been arriving first due at everything from a first to a fifth alarm. There are simply no surprises left. Thus, he does not consider it unusual to pick up a working fire enroute to quarters from a previously transmitted false alarm. No one in the area had concerned themselves with sending in an alarm for this particular fire, but this doesn't seem odd to Cullen. Failure to bother with such mundane pursuits is part of the Harlem mystique.

Cullen's reactions are instinctive; basically, they're honed by the repetition of a thousand similar situations. His report via radio is short and to the point, and his instructions to his subordinates are precise and clearly understood.

The huge cloud of billowing smoke obscures the involved building. It's not until the apparatus has pulled directly in front of the structure that Cullen realizes he's confronted with a brownstone and its numerous hazards. Smoke pours from every window and scantily clad occupants, clutching the barest of possessions, flee the building. Since the building is occupied as a rooming house, the captain surmises correctly that the population of this relatively small building will be large.

Cullen heads into the interior accompanied by Henderson. The physical punishment this pair is about to absorb will be brutal. Henderson is equipped with a 2½ gallon extinguisher and will use this device's limited capacity pending the arrival of an engine company. They'll search as much of the interior as will be humanly possible. In the process, they'll gamble their lives in an effort to save people they've never met, or will ever meet.

Cullen will have no concern regarding the actions of the balance of his crew. They've been down this road before and they'll perform professionally. Accompanied by Henderson, he crawls down a long, smoke-filled hallway, towards a dim glow at the end of the hall.

As soon as he'd braked the apparatus to a halt, Silensa had leaped to the operating table. He'd glanced over the side and observed Gillian dropping and securing the supporting chocks. John had raised the aerial to the roof and headed in that direction followed by Gillian.

People trapped at rear windows will be the primary concern of this pair. Equipped with life belts and a roof rope, these two firefighters represent the sole possibility of survival for any person trapped in the upper reaches of this doomed building. The climb to the roof takes no more than fifteen seconds. Ten seconds later they're peering over the roof. There's an hysterically screaming woman leaning out of a smoke-filled window.

Pudgy Dunn and Willie Burrell were removing a 25 ′ ladder from the side of the apparatus before the aerial reached the roof. Raising the device in seconds, they'd maneuvered it to a second-story window. Assisting a young mother and her three small children to the street was a piece of cake, but getting inside the window to search this ghastly interior is another matter. It's Willie who hears the gasping, strangled sound. The heat is terrible, the smoke and fumes unbearable. Flames are starting to light up over their heads. The window and the ladder leading to the street are invitingly close. They crowd towards the whimpering sound.

As he crawls down the hallway behind Captain Cullen, Tom Henderson is not unmindful of the constant advice of his wife concerning a transfer out of Harlem. The glow at the end of the hallway is increasing and the fumes directly overhead are starting to light up. Henderson uses the extinguisher's pitifully inadequate stream towards the ceiling. The effects are negligible. The stifling, choking effects of the fumes are slowing Henderson down and he's becoming disoriented. He gets as low as possible and seeks a bit of oxygen. He can hear the captain calling. He must need help. Henderson tries to push forward but it's like trying to run on a feather mattress. He can still hear the captain but now it's as if from a great distance. The heat is unbearable and the smoke as thick and oppressive as ever. He'll rest for a moment, then he'll push on. Just one moment's rest . . . just one moment . . . just one moment.

Jim Gillian is a man possessed of brute strength, so it's only natural that he'd tie a bowline and a bight and secure it on John Silensa. It would be just as natural to lower John over the roof in an attempt to rescue the hysterically screaming female. Reversing the process and requiring Silensa to cope with his 250 pounds would hardly be practical.

They'd whipped off sufficient rope from the reel for the job, but there simply wasn't time to search through the dense clouds of smoke for a chimney or other device sturdy enough to anchor the rope. Taking the required three turns through the hook of his life belt, Jim had lowered Silensa over the side with a fervent prayer.

He knew when John had the woman because the extra weight pulled him towards the edge of the roof. It was at that moment that Jim cursed the long departed architect who had designed the brownstone. There was a parapet on three sides of the roof. The rear, flat as a pancake, led directly into space. Slowly and surely the descending Silensa and the rescued woman drag Gillian towards the edge of the roof. Straining with all his might, the huge man struggles to hold his ground. Inch by inch he's hauled to the roof's edge. He has to hold on. He has to hold on. He has to.

As he reaches the window, John has a moment of panic. There's no one there. Could they have screwed up? Picked the wrong window? Has the woman jumped?

The smoke is billowing through the window and John can see the room starting to light up. He kicks out the remaining pieces of glass and enters the room. The woman lies on the floor and Silensa has one hell of a time lifting the victim to his shoulder. Slowly he steps through the window and swings into space. His descent is slow for a time. Suddenly he starts to pick up speed. The rate of descent is much too fast.

Easy, Jim. Not so fast. There's still a long way to go. It's no time for a nasty drop. John thinks of his wife and kids. For God's sake—take it easy, Jim—not so fast. Please, Jim—please.

Ray Cullen has taken many a pounding in his long career but none as bad as this. This one's the all-time prize winner. He holds his hand over his head and it almost blisters. The overhead atmosphere is becoming supercharged. He's sure that this place will be lighting up soon.

He crawls forward inch by inch. He has his flashlight on, sweeping the area, and finally spots a huddled form. He moves forward as rapidly as possible and finally reaches the victim. He turns the body over. It's an elderly woman and she's frightfully overweight. There isn't the semblance of muscle tone and it's like trying to pick up three hundred pounds of feathers. No matter how hard he tries, he can't budge the victim. "Tom, get your ass up here! I can't handle her alone!"

The area is starting to light up. "Tom, for the love of God, man! Where are you?" The captain turns in panic. There's no one near him. How does he handle this situation? If he stays, he dies. If he leaves, he'll never be able to live with himself. "Help me! Some one help me!"

There's no answer. No answer at all.

As Willie Burrell crawls towards the whimpering sound, he can feel Pudgy Dunn grasping at his turnout coat. He's reassured by Pudgy's presence. He sure as hell doesn't want to be alone in this environment. He bumps into something—furniture of a sort. He hears the crash of glass. He's knocked something over. "Sorry, tenants. Send the bill to Mayor Koch!"

He starts to laugh. The laughter, low at first, increases in intensity. He can't figure out what the hell he's laughing at since there sure isn't anything funny about this situation. He crawls forward a few more feet through the punishing atmosphere.

The whimpering sounds have ceased. Willie feels around in all directions—he's sure someone's here. They've got to keep looking. They've just got to keep looking.

While Pudgy Dunn regards himself as a man possessed of a sense of humor, he fails to see anything funny in the current situation. He's amazed that Willie Burrell could find something to laugh at. Pudgy's idea is to clear the area of occupants and get outside for a breath of reasonably fresh air.

"C'mon, Willie! What is this—a vaudeville fucking show? Let's cut the comedy and get the hell out of here!"

The fact that one of these Harlem jobs might finalize his career has, of course, occurred to Ray Cullen. While never really dwelling on the matter, he is aware of the hazards associated with his calling. Now, in the hallway of this Harlem brownstone, the possibility of meeting his Maker is strong. Very strong.

He's got a grip on this woman at last and is slowly dragging her down the hall. He's given up hope of any assistance from Henderson. He's sure the man's in trouble.

Help must arrive soon; the captain's strength is deteriorating rapidly and he's passed the stage where he can waste energy calling for help. Awhile back he'd thought of leaving the woman and coming back with assistance. He'd abandoned the idea as a cop-out. He brings her out or he stays with her. He has difficulty breathing. He feels ready to pass out. He's beginning to experience strange sensations. There comes a moment when he feels water. How could one feel water at a time like this? Where would the water come from? He lies still for a moment trying to gather strength, becoming aware of another presence. Engine 58 is pushing in with a line. The troops have arrived.

Cullen feels himself being dragged to the rear. He tries to protest. They can't leave that woman. They've got to search the area for Henderson. *Wait a minute, guys! Let me explain . . . let me explain . . . let me explain.*

Gillian wasn't more than six inches from the edge of the roof when the slackened rope indicated Silensa's arrival in the rear yard of the brownstone. He'd hardly had time to breathe a sigh of relief when he'd spotted yet another victim. And this one apparently resented the vicissitudes of life.

A middle-aged man was hanging out a window and loudly berating what he considered the cowardly actions of the New York City Fire Department. He demanded relief from his predicament in language far from elegant.

Jim hauled up the rope and tied the slack end to a vent pipe that looked far from secure. Leaving the rope hanging free, Jim attached the rope to his life belt and slid to the trapped man. He instructed him to wrap his arms and legs in a manner making the rescue possible.

While Gillian didn't expect a vote of confidence, neither did he expect abuse. "You motherfucker! What the hell kept you so long?"

Willie Burrell has finally found the victim. The little old lady huddled at the rear of the room doesn't weigh more than eighty pounds. Willie shoulders the unconscious woman and scurries to the window. He's followed by Pudgy.

Willie is out of the window in a moment, but Pudgy takes a bit longer. Encountering what he thought was a pile of clothing, Pudgy investigated further. Pudgy wasn't concerned at all that he'd found an unconscious dog. As long as he had nothing better to do, he might as well rescue a dog. All in a day's work. All in a day's work.

There were eleven families associated with this Harlem brownstone. Four victims leaped to their deaths into the rear yard prior to the arrival of Ladder 26. The other seven were found in the variety of rooms rented by the owner.

Seventeen persons were rescued by the responding firefighters operating at this second alarm, but this had little effect on Battalion Chief McCarthy. He's a man possessed of an infinite capacity for criticism.

The four persons lying in the backyard aggravated him to no end. The fact that they were dead prior to the arrival of Ladder 26 failed to mollify him. He even chose to ignore Ladder 14's use of the life net to rescue eight others. He's not overly enthusiastic concerning the truly heroic efforts of Gillian and Silensa. He's aggravated by this pair and Captain Cullen as well. The stubborn insistence of all the personnel assigned to Ladder 26 in using the Manila rescue rope has McCarthy outraged. McCarthy regards Cullen's total distrust of the newly assigned nylon rope as asinine. He's made up his mind. The Manila rope will be removed from the apparatus of Ladder 26. And McCarthy regards Captain Cullen's insistence on writing up Gillian and Silensa for citations as childish. The efforts of Engine 58, Engine 35 and Engine 36 in the removal of potential victims he believes hardly worthy of mention.

For some unusual reason McCarthy is wildly enthused by the actions of Pudgy Dunn, and Dunn is truly embarrassed. He regards Pudgy's rescue of the dog as heroic and insists on Pudgy posing for a host of shots by arriving news photographers. He's even mentioned something about a medal from some humane society.

Pudgy's opinion of Chief McCarthy is another matter: "I'm sick and tired of that jerk! I wish someone would transfer him to Staten-Fucking-Island!"

The Adversaries

It's understandable that circumstances alter cases. Since any action can cause a reaction, it's natural that the brownstone fire had an effect on the members of the Fire Factory. Actually, the use of the word "reaction" is rather mild. In this particular instance "catastrophe" is more appropriate, at least as it concerned firefighters Tom Henderson and Harry Alcock.

The end of the Damon and Pythias relationship that existed between Henderson and Alcock took the other men by surprise. They'd been buddies for such a long time that the developing feud was difficult to rationalize. Lieutenant Anderson could hardly believe his ears when Alcock approached him. "I'd like a new group assignment. Working with that son-of-a-bitch Henderson is just too much."

Described variously as "pals," "ass-hole buddies," "the Rosedale twins" and a host of additional descriptive verbiage indicating closeness, Henderson and Alcock had been regarded as inseparable. They'd even conspired to spend their vacations together. While there may be nothing unusual about arranging similar vacations in the outside world, it's a whole other ball game in the world of the fire department. In order to insure fairness, vacations are rotated. If a man agrees to swap an August vacation for the frigid February atmosphere, that's his business. The venture may even be profitable. Exchanging a vacation for monetary consideration is not unheard of.

It's the way this pair went about insuring similar vacations that sets them apart. The amount of skulduggery, arm twisting, petty bribery and overt threats utilized to obtain their ends has been close to scandalous. To quote Gillian, "I'm afraid to draw a summer vacation. It might be worth my life to interfere with the travel plans of those scheming bastards."

Gillian's fears have merit, even if somewhat exaggerated. Alcock and Henderson did put in an inordinate amount of time planning an exotic variety of family vacations.

Paradoxically, the larceny involved in the vacation exchanges is not what bugs the members of these Harlem units. After all, they do have a choice. They *could* say *no*. It's the backwash associated with these periods that drives these firefighters up the wall. Their trip to Florida's Disney World and Larry Fitzmaurice's reaction to that vacation may serve as an example. "If I see one more goddamned picture of those two families and that idiot Mickey Mouse, I'm gonna puke!" Nor was Oscar Ratner's reaction concerning the family movies of the Alcock-Henderson trip to Yellow Stone National Park less different: "I kept hoping that friggin' grizzly bear would eat one of their kids."

The fact that Oscar, a man constantly in debt, had swapped his August vacation for a fast fifty may have some bearing on the matter. The second thoughts he'd had during the February period originally assigned to Alcock provides sufficient additional speculation. "That bastard's name should be ALLBALLS. I almost froze my ass off on that vacation."

It's rather odd that the mindless dispute between this pair should start with Alcock actually saving Henderson's life. The fact that a man assigned to an engine company seldom has the opportunity to rescue a fellow human may well have something to do with the situation.

The feud started with the fire in the brownstone on 120th Street just off Fifth Avenue. The engine company members, on returning to quarters from the false alarm at Madison Avenue and 122nd Street, were wondering just what the hell was delaying the truck's return. The fact that the dispatcher had a host of traffic to handle may have been responsible for the five-minute delay between Captain Cullen's original report and the transmission of the alarm. Regardless of circumstances, Engine 58's personnel were well aware they were going to work when they'd turned left on 120th Street. The smoke was so thick they could barely see the apparatus of Ladder 26. The only members of that unit visible were Willie Burrell and Pudgy Dunn, and not surprisingly these two were busily removing a woman and three small children from a first story window. What was even less surprising was the manner in which these men routinely disappeared into the smoke-filled room for further search.

There had been a host of rescues at that fire ranging from Gillian and Silensa's rooftop exploits to Pudgy's removal of an occupant's dog. Everything had been taken in stride, as rescue work is undoubtedly the job's number one priority.

Since the hallway to this relatively small building was not very wide, it was only natural that the members of Engine 58 would stumble over the inert forms of Captain Cullen, Fireman Henderson and the enormously fat lady the captain had managed to drag some ten feet down the hall.

Lieutenant Anderson had occupied himself with operating the nozzle while his crew removed the variety of unconscious forms. The new kid, Jack McBride, dragged out the captain while Murray and Fitzmaurice cursed and swore vigorously as they removed the unconscious female. Since it would be uncharacteristic for Fitzmaurice to labor in silence, his comments had been eloquent. "What the fuck have we got here? It must be a goddamned hippopotamus."

That was all that Fitzmaurice had to say, and if Alcock could have followed suit, his feud with Henderson would never have occurred. He had removed Henderson, however, and had been so overcome with his own prowess that he discussed the matter at considerable length.

The captain and Henderson had been taken to St. Luke's Hospital. Alcock called Henderson's wife and let her know Tom's condition. He also made damned sure the woman knew who'd saved her husband. He also dwelt on the matter at the bedside of Henderson the following morning. This had resulted in the first unkind words.

Henderson hadn't expected Alcock to react in an hysterical manner in his expressions of sympathy. After all, Henderson's prognosis was far from critical. He did, however, feel his friend might at least have asked him how he felt before going into graphic descriptions of his own exploits.

Henderson had a vicious headache. He'd have loved a cup of coffee, something the doctors had placed off limits pending a variety of tests. As Alcock went on and on about the density of the smoke, the length of the hallway and the variety of hazards associated with removing a victim in such perilous circumstances, Henderson, for the first time, wondered if his friend might have been vaccinated with a phonograph needle.

Finally raising himself on an elbow, he looked directly at Alcock. "What the fuck is it you want? Do you expect the Congressional Medal of Honor? That goddamned hallway couldn't have been more than twenty feet long and it was on the ground floor. They won't even write you up. It was strictly routine, so cut out the bullshit!"

Alcock had been hurt—deeply hurt. That his lifelong friend could react in such an ungracious manner was amazing. It had been unfortunate that Captain Cullen, occupying the adjoining bed, had been asleep. An old pro like Cullen would have calmed the pair down. He wasn't awake, Henderson was coffeeless and so the issue was joined.

As he walked toward the door leading to the hospital corridor, Alcock pointed toward Henderson and let him know his considered opinion of his former pal's attitude. "Fuck you, Henderson! The next time I leave you right where you are and save my own ass!" Henderson's reply settled matters. "What 'next time,' you silly bastard? Rescues by guys assigned to engine companies come once in a lifetime. You've just had yours!"

It is unfortunate, and at the same time indicative of life's realities, that the wives of these two men should be responsible for deepening the feud. These sensible ladies were aware of the childish dispute and conspired to get their husbands back on the right track. They'd finally come up with a scheme designed to end this nonsense. Why not insist on Alcock driving the recovered invalid back to work? After all, they had car pooled for years. Surely this would give them time to shake hands and make up.

A marvelous plan, but one with a fly in the ointment. Captain Cullen was still on medical leave and Jim Gillian was filling in as Acting Lieutenant. Scatterbrained, as usual, Gillian had assumed Henderson would be returning to his old work group. Unfortunately, the battalion had expressed other thoughts in a written memo lying unread on the office desk of Ladder 26.

The memo was still laying undisturbed when Alcock and Henderson arrived in Harry's ancient station wagon. Alcock wasn't keen on making up. He still felt rather put upon. While he felt unworthy of the Congressional Medal of Honor as suggested by that wise guy Henderson, he sure as hell was feeling shortchanged. The guy still hadn't said thanks. Henderson was in a similar mood. He's in this car to keep peace with the wife. If he hears any further comments concerning alleged rescues, he'll peel Alcock's hide strip by strip.

They'd walked into the firehouse together and it was Lieutenant Anderson who'd started the fur flying. "Hey, Henderson! What the hell brings you here tonight? You're not due in until tomorrow at 6:00 p.m."

Indicative of the paranoia afflicting the pair during this period of turmoil, Henderson immediately assumed Alcock had deliberately brought him to work twenty-four hours early. Glaring in Harry's direction, he'd lost little time in expressing an opinion. "You stink, Alcock!"

Alcock was amazed. "How come I stink?" Stepping back, Henderson blasted his former buddy with both barrels. "You stink because only a first-class prick would deliberately bring a guy to work twenty-four hours early!"

Henderson's blasphemous comments concerning former friends fell on unbelieving ears. That this guy would actually accuse him of being miserable enough to shaft a man fresh out of a sick bed by bringing him to work a day early was just too much. For this ingrate to fail to acknowledge the gift of life was one thing, but to accuse him falsely was another matter. He felt obliged to answer. "Keep it up, Henderson, and you'll be right back in the hospital!"

Actually, it was the presence of Lieutenant Anderson that prevented the pair from rolling all over the apparatus floor.

They were that angry. To Henderson's outraged demands as to how he'd get all the way back to Rosedale, Alcock had a one-word solution: "WALK." Henderson had other ideas. Walking simply wasn't part of his game plan. Alcock had forgotten one small item. For all the years they'd been buddies, each man kept a set of the other's car keys. It had been a convenience on many an occasion. For Henderson it would be a convenience one more time.

Henderson removed Alcock's car from its parking space and drove home. Once there he lost little time phoning Alcock. Momentarily Alcock was confused and wondered why this ingrate was calling him. He soon found out. Henderson's advice concerning heavy shoes and a good pair of socks to ease the walk from Harlem to Rosedale sent Alcock into a tirade that was shocking even to Billy Murray. Billy's observation that he'd thought he'd heard all the words was lost on Alcock. He was too busy planning revenge. He wasn't even aware of Murray's presence.

Captain Cullen returned to duty a week later. One of his first acts was to see that Henderson was reassigned to his old group. Feud or no feud, Henderson was the type of guy Cullen wanted working with him. A little pressure applied to the battalion and the captain had his way. He was sure that the situation between the warring Alcock and Henderson would straighten itself out shortly. He was wrong.

It was Thursday, the traditional horse playing day for the former buddies. Alcock had procured a scratch sheet and had deliberately left it on the kitchen table. Henderson walked right into the trap. Stepping toward the scratch sheet he'd picked it up. The sheet was promptly snatched from his hands. "That's private property. Keep your hands off it!"

"Shove it up your ass!" was the only comment Henderson could think of. He'd have liked to come up with something really devastating—something to crush this pseudo hero—but he couldn't think of a thing. He was simply too embarrassed. Fully aware that Alcock had set him up, Henderson planned revenge. The fact that he couldn't come up with a decent idea, something that would really embarrass Alcock, depressed him.

Given the normal odds, Alcock would have picked a horse scheduled to go down the drain. After all, the combined race track skill of this pair of combatants hadn't produced an outstanding winner in the memory of man. Surely Alcock's selections would lead to the inevitable out-of-the-money finish. They didn't. He spotted a horse entered in the seventh at Aqueduct that was saddled with the highly improbable name "Rascally Tom." Alcock regarded this as an omen. The fact that the horse was a six-year-old maiden listed at 30-1 concerned him not at all.

Extremely cautious men by nature, Alcock and Henderson had never wagered more than a dollar apiece in all the years they'd played the horses. Ratner's caustic comments concerning guys stupid enough to spend more money on scratch sheets than they actually wagered wasn't far from the mark.

On this particular day Alcock, throwing caution to the winds, had placed twenty dollars on Rascally Tom's nose. He regarded it as simple justice when the horse came in paying telephone numbers. If he wasn't to be cited for saving the life of the two-legged Rascally Tom, it was only fair and equitable that the four-legged variety reward him properly.

He made it his business to see that the $620 from the local bookie was converted to one dollar bills. His insistence on counting the pile over and over came close to driving Henderson mad. "Think you're pretty smart, don't you?" The remark hardly caused an interruption in Alcock's monotonous count. "I'm the guy with this pile of money in front of him, so I know how smart I am!"

This obvious logic drove Henderson out of the kitchen and down into the basement where he proceeded to punch the wall. The resultant pain increased his determination to get back at that bastard Alcock.

Henderson thought and he thought and he thought. For all his thought, however, he couldn't come up with a single plan. Finally his revenge arrived even though Henderson personally had nothing to do with getting back at Alcock. His oldest son went to bat for him.

Alcock had done considerable talking around the house in the presence of his kids. The results were clearly predictable.

Johnny Alcock found it necessary to inform his friend, Billy Henderson, concerning his father's shortcomings. "My father saved your father's life! Your father wasn't even nice enough to say thank you!"

The shiner hung on Johnny Alcock by Billy Henderson was a thing of lasting beauty. It stayed around for three weeks, remaining a sheer swollen black for an interval of time. Gradually the eye changed to a kaleidoscopic pattern of orange, yellow, purple and red. Every time Henderson saw Johnny, he laughed and laughed and laughed. He laughed a full $620 worth.

Naturally things around the firehouse were not the same. Fitzmaurice's attempt to peddle his August vacation were unsuccessful. Alcock's nasty suggestion that Fitzie "stick his vacation in his ear" was hardly conducive to maintaining neighborly relations. Nor was Gillian's attempt to do business with Henderson any more profitable. Henderson's "I have better things to do with my money than waste it on the likes of you" was regarded as most inhospitable by Jim.

There's simply no way of knowing how far this childish charade would have continued. Fate finally stepped in and brought Alcock and Henderson to their senses. One night when Alcock was not at home, one of his youngsters came close to choking to death at the supper table. A fast scream across the yard brought Henderson speeding to the rescue. Applying the proper techniques, he had the child breathing normally in no time at all.

Naturally the feud was at an end as far as the pair were concerned. The rest of the firehouse would be another matter. Sooner or later Alcock and Henderson would be around questioning Fitzmaurice and Gillian concerning their vacations. It won't happen tomorrow or the next day, but they'll be around. To quote Fitzie: "I hope that bastard Alcock hasn't spent all of that six hundred and twenty bucks." Fitzie has great plans for that money. His ambitions in that direction are almost as grandiose as Gillian's. Henderson will find Big Jim's August vacation expensive this year—very expensive.

Jim Gillian

Firefighters, like cops, postmen, pilots, sanitation workers and file clerks, spring from a variety of backgrounds. Divergence is the word that comes to mind. While some Fire Factory members emerge from the very Harlem tenements they protect, others are the products of neighborhoods far removed from ghetto areas.

Jim Gillian is not a Harlem product. Truthfully, he's not even from New York City. Garbage cans and smelly tenements were alien to Jim prior to his arrival in Harlem. He's a different man from the rest of the crew assigned to these units.

Actually, the world is a rather complex place for Jim Gillian. He's six-foot-five in a society populated by people inches shorter, and he's paid the price levied on the oversized. "I'm sick and tired of paying through the nose for size seventeen shoes!" His concerns are hardly limited to outrageous prices. He's also cursed with a tendency to put on weight, and his complaints on this subject are loud and vociferous. "That son-of-a-bitch Henderson could eat a horse without putting on an ounce!" Gillian's feelings regarding adding weight by merely picking up a menu have a legitimacy of a sort. When he's on a diet, he may tip the scales at 250; when off his diet, 300 is not outside the realm of possibility.

He's controversial by nature and it's understandable that matters other than diet and prices might concern him. Politics bother him. "Who am I supposed to vote for? I've got a choice between Howdy Doody and Clarabelle the Clown." Graffiti annoys him. "Any moron caught defacing a subway car should be forced to listen to Howard Cosell." Traffic outrages him. "That fuckin' Major Deegan Expressway should be blasted off the face of the earth!" The United Nations depresses him. "Name one thing useful that pack of pansies has accomplished."

Given this tendency toward controversy, it's hardly likely Gillian would agree with his fellow firefighters on all issues—or even a few, for that matter. He's intellectually gifted—head and shoulders over his peers in matters of the mind. "No, you dopey bastard, you cannot borrow money from the World Bank. You have to be a nation to pick Uncle Sam's pocket in that fashion." Again, artistically, Gillian outstrips his peers. He's an ardent opera buff and suffers deeply at the sense of musical ignorance exhibited by the likes of Fitzmaurice and Ratner. "You ignorant bastards. You know damned well Carmen doesn't operate a pizza parlor!"

While certainly not the first person of superior mental attainment to enter the department, Gillian is at least unusual in that respect. He's a surprisingly gifted athlete and had received a football scholarship to one of the larger universities. Since the NFL is constantly on the lookout for men of size and speed, it was not unusual that Gillian attracted the interests of a variety of professional scouts. He'd been good enough to hang on at Green Bay for two years before being cut. Then there'd been the service and Vietnam. Discharged from the army and newly married, he found that the fire department offered security in a world seemingly unaware of the problems confronting a veteran pushing thirty.

Gillian's a man of many accomplishments. After his appointment to the fire department, he'd constructed his own home in a community north of the Bronx. He put months on end into the project and he'd come up with a house of surprising beauty. Anyone knowing the man would not be surprised that the home would be complete in all respects save one. For all his mental accomplishments, Gillian is remarkably absent-minded. He'd actually forgotten to have his property's title searched. Consequently, he built a portion of his home on someone else's lot. This lapse of memory had cost him two thousand dollars. "The miserable bastard. A regular Archie

Bunker!"

Since he lives outside the city limits, it's natural that a good deal of Gillian's time is spent on a variety of highways connecting Westchester County and Harlem. Because he's so absent-minded, Gillian occasionally finds himself at home when he belongs at work. "That bloody work chart. It'd take a Philadelphia lawyer to figure out the goddamned thing!" His superiors are not overly impressed when he balances matters by showing up for work when he belongs at home.

The primary beneficiaries of Gillian's absent-minded tendencies are the variety of body and fender shops lining his route of travel. He's a notoriously poor driver, and when he's heading for Harlem in response to yet another work chart foul up, he's been involved in a dozen fender benders, numerous traffic tickets and an abiding, vitriolic dislike of anyone even remotely associated with any police department. "Fuckin' moron! I showed him my shield and he gives me a lecture on my moral responsibilities."

Police officers are not the only bone of contention in Gillian's hectic sphere of activity. Neighbors cause him concern. "The bastard is a Princeton graduate and feels a firefighter tends to lower property values." It never crosses Gillian's mind that his neighbor might have legitimate cause for concern. The Princeton graduate is a dog fancier and had secured a pedigreed Afghan hound. The man had plans for breeding the hound with an eye on the lucrative market in Afghan pups. Somehow Gillian's pride and joy, a mongrel showing evidence of seven or eight breeds, had gained access to the neighbor's property. Of course, the Afghan bitch was in heat on this particular occasion. Gillian regarded the situation as ludicrous: "Ya shoulda seen them pups! Ugliest goddamned bastards you'd ever lay eyes on!"

All things considered, it seems natural that Gillian would be involved in a feud with his in-laws. He'd married a girl of surpassing beauty but he cannot abide any member of her family: "Homeliest looking bunch of shits on the North American continent." The fact that Gillian is firmly convinced his wife had been involved in a baby switch at the hospital does little to calm the murky waters surrounding relations with his in-laws. "No way she could be related to that tribe. She has a brother in the police department that makes Oscar Ratner look like Clark Gable!"

Gillian's rather civic minded, and so he found it necessary to enroll in the volunteer fire department protecting his community. Gillian chose to regard as irrelevant that the "vollies" are social minded individuals with a fondness for beer. His wife, burdened with the responsibility of two small children and a husband seldom at home, objected strenuously. "If you're not at one firehouse or another, you're down at Delehanty's studying for promotion. I'm tired of being stuck in this house for days on end!"

Gillian was on the horns of a dilemma. He was unwilling to give up his friends at the vollies and he racked his mind for a solution. For days he gave the matter his undivided attention. How to get back in the good graces of "Honey"? How to have his cake and eat it? Finally, he came up with a solution.

From his earliest college days Gillian has been a prolific note taker. Everything uttered by the instructors at Delehantys is copied and filed for future reference. He also takes notes when attending meetings at the local volunteer fire department. Whether he refers to these notes, or even pays the vaguest attention to them is debatable.

On one particular occasion the persons in charge of Gillian's volunteer group decided to hold a discussion concerning an annual fund-raising affair. Out came Gillian's notebook. Since the affair in question concerned running a stag show for men only, it follows that Gillian could not have been paying too much attention. Either that or he had taken on a larger than usual quantity of beer. Arriving home he'd grandiosely informed Honey that he'd seen the light. "You're absolutely right, baby. You're in the house too much. I'm taking you to the racket that the vollies are throwing on Saturday night!"

For Honey the week had been a beehive of activity. Trips to the beauty parlor, a new pair of shoes and the hiring of a baby sitter were only the beginning. She's gifted with a ravishing figure and completed her ensemble by borrowing a mink coat from her sister. The sister was married to a doctor, a never-ending source of amazement to Gillian. "The guy must be blind. That broad's as ugly as sin!"

When this lovely creature stepped out of Gillian's car, the assembled vollies had assumed that this was the girl who would be leaping from the cake. They swept down on Honey, groping her in a variety of places strictly reserved for Gillian. The results were stupendous. Gillian was outraged at such undue familiarity and he laid about with a vengeance. Vollies were flying in all directions, some rising to stagger to safety, while others lay precisely where they'd fallen.

It took a half hour to sort out the matter. When he realized his asininity, Gillian had momentarily debated a career with the French Foreign Legion or possible suicide. The ride home had been a classic. Honey persisted in beating Gillian about the head with her pocketbook. "One of those animals actually yanked off my bra!"

As Gillian debated the possibility of coming close to Honey's brassiere—or anything else of an intimate nature—he made up his mind. No more volunteers. He'd stay the hell away from those guys. At least the men in Harlem would have brains enough not to confuse a swell gal like Honey with some stripteaser. Gillian had regarded as superfluous the fact that the vollies hadn't met his wife.

He was sure that this was the answer. He would give strict attention to his paying job. He would devote lots of time to studying for advancement. He would even try to make up with the Princeton graduate. After all, wasn't he a college man himself? As he steered in the direction of home, he'd made up his mind to be a better driver. He'd seen the light. No more accidents.

The similarity to New Year's Eve occurred to Jim. Never had he made so many resolutions. He was sure he'd keep them. No more arguing with the guys in the Harlem firehouse. After all, they are a swell bunch.

It's a certainty he'll turn over a new leaf, with one exception. There's no way he'll accept that ugly bunch of in-laws. The miserable bastards. No way he'll accept them at all. That would be asking too much.

Oscar

If Gillian rates a mention as a personality, Oscar Ratner cannot be ignored. He's one of a kind, this Fire Factory natural, and for this the officer personnel of every other firehouse in New York City breathe a sigh of relief. Lieutenant Anderson is stuck with this gift from the gods—Lieutenant Anderson who curses his fate on a daily basis.

Oscar Ratner is a paradox to Anderson. The lieutenant can find no other way of describing the man. For months on end his behavior will be normal. It will be sufficiently circumspect to warrant a merit badge. Since Engine 58 is far from a boy scout troop, the occasions when Oscar functions in the manner required by rules and regulations must go unrewarded. It's not that Lieutenant Anderson wouldn't create a prize of some sort to keep Oscar on the straight and narrow. It's not that at all. It's the utter unpredictability of the man that drives the lieutenant to distraction. When will he strike next? In what bizarre episode will he involve himself? How will his latest shenanigans affect the unit? Will his variety of pecadilloes reach the ears of the brass? Will there be a reaction?

In his many conversations with Captain Cullen concerning Fireman Ratner, and whatever outrageous adventure he may have involved himself, Lieutenant Anderson had become adamant on one point. "I only wish the son of a bitch was a boozer. If the guy drank, I could tie him up in the cellar. There's a predictability about a drunk. That I could handle. Oscar Ratner is a fuckin' psycho!"

There's simply no telling what will turn the quixotic Ratner from the normally functioning Motor Pump Operator of

Engine 58 into a candidate for the rubber room at Bellevue. Take his dislike for Battalion Chief McCarthy, a not unusual reaction since everyone dislikes McCarthy. It's the way Oscar goes about expressing his animosity, however, that's unusual. While the average man would mumble to himself concerning his opinion of this frightfully obnoxious character, Oscar is more direct.

His conflict with McCarthy started with the fire in the supermarket on 116th Street near Lenox Avenue. In his usual inimitable manner the chief had found fault with every aspect of the operation. Nothing, absolutely nothing, had pleased him. He chose to regard the fact that the fire had been held to an all hands job, despite the obvious potential for a greater alarm, as superfluous.

While it's probable that many members of various ranks had thoughts concerning this despicable character, it had been Oscar who seized the bull by the horns. Outside the fire department it's entirely possible Oscar's conduct in the matter might be regarded as rather ordinary. However, since department operations are conducted on a semi-military basis, the disparity in rank made Ratner's actions insane to say the least.

Oscar approached as McCarthy was in the process of informing a member of the press about his chiefly expertise in saving that part of Harlem from disaster. Oscar had a question. "Hey, chief, how come you're such a prick?"

To say that McCarthy's reaction was catastrophic would be putting the matter mildly. His original intent was to fling seven charges at Ratner ranging from "Violating his oath of office" to "Conduct unbecoming a member of the department."

The union forced the issue. Since an election was in the offing, it hadn't been difficult to convince City Hall of the inadvisability of rubbing firefighters the wrong way. McCarthy was forced to settle for a lesser penalty and Oscar was required to perform three extra watch tours. Realistically, it was a penalty Oscar felt capable of performing while standing on one leg.

When asked why he'd bothered to ask the chief such a question, Oscar's answer had been simple: "I was curious." It wasn't the only time his curiosity got him into trouble. At the annual Holy Name Society communion breakfast Oscar saw fit to approach McCarthy while the chief was waxing holy in front of the department chaplains. He was curious. He had a question to ask. "Tell me, chief, were you ever at a fire before you were assigned to Harlem?"

Since McCarthy's firefighting experience had been limited to a brief tenure in a remote section of Staten Island, Oscar's barb found its mark. Actually, McCarthy had been detailed to the School of Instruction as a lieutenant and captain, finally losing his detail with his promotion to Battalion Chief. There was much speculation whether he'd ever operated a nozzle or used a six-foot hook.

Oscar's additional watches brought happiness of a sort to Fitzmaurice and Brennan who were of a mind to feed him questions designed to outrage the chief. Their rationale that Oscar on watch gave them more sack time meant nothing to Ratner. Since Billy Murray regards the late watches as an excellent opportunity for study, Oscar merely signed the book and went back upstairs to bed.

After being zapped by McCarthy for the second time, Oscar acted in a surprisingly normal manner for a remarkably long period. He arrived on time for work. He performed housewatch duty in a competent manner. His maintenance of apparatus in quarters and at fires was thoroughly professional.

There were those inclined to believe Oscar had learned his lesson insofar as horsing around with Chief McCarthy was concerned. Lieutenant Anderson, however, was not one so inclined. Like the light sleeper who waits for his upstairs neighbor to drop the other shoe, so Anderson anticipated Oscar's next outrage on the unpopular McCarthy. "That crazy son of a bitch is acting too normal. It can't last."

The lieutenant was right. It couldn't last. Oscar's fall from grace occurred while the unit was performing apparatus field inspection duty on Fifth Avenue in the vicinity of 118th Street. Billy Murray had encountered a situation that required the attention of Lieutenant Anderson. When the pair had disappeared into the tenement, Oscar had felt lonesome, but the feeling didn't last for long.

It was not unusual for the apparatus to be parked directly in front of number 1440 Fifth Avenue. Nor was the rather swinging party taking place in one of the ground floor apartments of that particular building anything out of the ordinary. There are plenty of parties in Harlem. Any number of persons regard Harlem as one continuous party. Since he's been in the area for over twenty-two years, Oscar felt not the slightest bit bashful about checking out the festivities.

If Lieutenant Anderson had abesnted himself from the apparatus for some five minutes, that's precisely the length of time Oscar would have had to celebrate with his new-found friends. Unfortunately, the lieutenant and Billy Murray had become involved with a boisterous and volatile superintendent who obviously had no intentions of accepting the summons prepared by these representatives of the fire department. "Man, you can take that motherfucker summons and stick it in your ear!"

The lieutenant had no intention of sticking the summons in his ear. Nor would he allow Billy Murray the privilege of bouncing the super against the wall. The situation required tact and diplomacy on the lieutenant's part, but unfortunately tact and diplomacy take time. That time was filled by Chief McCarthy's arrival alongside the apparatus of Engine 58.

The chief's car had arrived as silently as possible since it was McCarthy's intention to find Lieutenant Anderson goofing off outside one of the buildings, a position he was firmly convinced Anderson assumed as often as possible.

While he may have been disappointed at the Lieutenant's absence, he was totally dumbfounded to find the apparatus in the complete control of some fourteen kids ranging in age from four to twelve. The kids had simply taken advantage of the opportunity to play fireman. They'd stretched two lengths of hose into the street and were theatrically dousing an imaginary fire. Several of them were up on the apparatus pointing the deck pipe at the same imaginary conflagration. Still another sat in the driver's seat. One of the more enterprising had discovered how to operate the radio and was industriously breaking the outraged dispatcher's chops.

While the chief may have been disappointed at Anderson's absence, he was beside himself with rage on spotting Oscar dancing up a storm with a local mama of some 220 pounds. Certainly the average firefighter would never have involved himself in such a spectacle. It's equally certain the reactions of any other member involved in such an embarrassing situation would have been different. Ratner later explained that since he was about to be hung, he might as well swing for stealing the Queen's jewels rather than a loaf of bread. This made sense of a sort.

As he leaned out of the ground floor window Oscar had given an expert imitation of the television character Maxwell Smart. "Chief, would you believe I've been kidnapped? No! Well, in that case, would you believe I've been elected Mayor of Harlem? No! Well, would you believe I stopped in to take a leak? No! Well, in that case, would you believe I'm having the best fucking time I've had in a month!"

The brass threw out the chief's attempt to sock Lieutenant Anderson with departmental charges over the matter. Since the man had been precisely where he belonged, they rationalized there was no basis for action.

Oscar's case was another matter. This time the union couldn't get him off the hook. His departmental trial resulted in a five-day loss of pay and the temporary removal of his assignment as Motor Pump Operator.

When asked about his temporary loss of position as Motor Pump Operator, Oscar's reply ranged from the vulgar to the obscene. "Fuck it! Who needs it?" was perhaps the gentlest of his responses. He was verbally attacked by Alcock, who was outraged at being saddled with Oscar's former responsibility. Oscar's reply to this was practical and to the point: "You want off the hook? It's easy! Tell that crumbum McCarthy what you really think of him and you're home free!"

Release from the responsibility of handling the apparatus seemed to endow Oscar with a new lease on life as far as his social activities around the firehouse were concerned. The newfound freedom seemingly gave him time for a variety of options not previously explored. He descended into the basement area where he proceeded to disturb the resident karate experts. He almost drove them up the wall with his annoying interruptions and caustic comments. Murray and Burrell were of a mind to hospitalize Oscar, and this feeling was forcibly brought to the attention of Lieutenant Anderson. "Lieutenant, that man calls me a faggot one more time and I ain't gonna be responsible for my actions!"

This complaint by the usually mild mannered Burrell was reason enough for the lieutenant to order Ratner from the basement area on a permanent basis. While Anderson's actions solved one problem, they created another.

Shifting his base of operations from cellar to kitchen, it took Oscar some ten minutes to inform Fitzmaurice that arm wrestling was a pastime for the decrepit. Head butting was the new macho sport—an activity to be indulged in by men and never by faggots. Seemingly, Oscar had become intrigued by the word faggot, to the point where he used it in every other sentence.

Always one to take a dare, Fitzie had accompanied Oscar to the apparatus floor where they'd proceeded to give an excellent imitation of two male mountain sheep attempting to remove competition during the mating season. They damn near removed one another. As Lieutenant Anderson later described the incident to Captain Cullen, his outrage had reached a new high. "They looked like a pair of fucking unicorns!"

Once again Anderson's orders had been clear: "No more head butting!" Always one to obey the latest order, Oscar refrained from head butting. After all, it gave him a headache and was probably an activity indulged in by faggots.

Lieutenant Anderson should have been more explicit. Since Oscar was in one of his insane cycles, the lieutenant should have touched all the bases. He didn't. If he had, it's entirely possible Oscar's next venture into the realm of the impossible could not have occurred.

It was Jim Gillian who set the scene. He'd been fascinated by a discussion with one of the older members concerning operations at fires without the use of masks. "How," he wondered, "did they manage?" As usual, Oscar had a solution. His contention that sticking one's head under water to strengthen one's breath-holding capacity led to a debate. Naturally, it also led to a wager.

On the following tour Oscar appeared with a large aluminum device remarkably similar to an old-time washtub. After filling the device with water, it seemed only proper that a few wagers should be made. Oscar had been practicing at home and he felt supremely confident that he could take his buddies over the hurdles. He did more than take them over the hurdles. Brennan damn near drowned.

As Lieutenant Anderson considered the utter impossibility of convincing any one in authority as to how one of his personnel could have drowned in the middle of Harlem, he also considered ways of killing Oscar. He was serious. "I'm telling you, Captain, that son of a bitch is driving me up the wall. If I can figure out a way, I'm gonna kill him."

The lieutenant didn't kill Oscar. He compromised by inviting him into the office for a royal chewing out. Ratner's reaction to Anderson's outburst became a topic of conversation among his peers. Since Oscar's conduct improved considerably, there were those firmly convinced the lieutenant's tongue-lashing had achieved its objective. "The lieutenant's got him scared shitless," was Fitzmaurice's assessment. Gillian disagreed. "Oscar is in one of his normal cycles. As soon as it's high tide or the moon is full, or whatever the hell it is that sets him off, Oscar will be as nutty as ever!"

Whether or not Gillian's collegiate career included a course in abnormal psychology is beside the point. He was right in his assessment of Ratner. After several weeks of rather normal behavior the tide rose, or the moon became full, and Oscar was off and running in search of the bizarre.

Once again, Engine 58 was performing apparatus field inspection duty in an area best left to the imagination. Cadly Hall was the name generously bestowed on the buildings under inspection, a Single Room Occupancy inhabited by welfare cases ranging from prostitutes no longer able to give it away to recently released mental incompetents. Cadly Hall represented an opportunity for Lieutenant Anderson to stick

58 The Fire Factory

it to Oscar.

It's debatable whether or not Oscar's subseqent actions were aimed at getting even with the lieutenant for assigning him this particular pesthole for inspection. Since the moon was full and the tide high, it's entirely possible Oscar's paranoia would have manifested itself in any event.

Mumbling to himself concerning the injustices inflicted on firefighters assigned to the Harlem area, Oscar had proceeded into the interior of the building. On reaching the third floor he'd encountered a situation unusual even for Cadly Hall. A gang bang was in progress. One of the more generous female residents was in the process of donating her sexual favors to anyone having the patience to wait in line. Naturally, this gave Oscar ideas.

As he proceeded to the street level with Lieutenant Anderson as his original target, Oscar had been overjoyed to encounter Chief McCarthy. The lieutenant had spotted the chief's car several blocks away and had scurried into one of the buildings. This left Alcock as Motor Pump Operator to deal with this obnoxious individual.

Playing his role to the hilt, Oscar breathlessly informed the chief about a stupendous pile of rubbish at the base of one of the shafts. Basically, McCarthy would have enjoyed nothing better than ordering Lieutenant Anderson to take appropriate action, but since the lieutenant wasn't available, McCarthy's only option was to accompany Oscar into the interior of Cadley Hall.

To say that McCarthy was uncomfortable is to state the obvious. It was difficult for Oscar to determine whether McCarthy was more concerned with physical assault or the possibility of infection. Oscar's later explanation was emphatic: "The son of a bitch stayed precisely two inches behind me from the moment we entered the building."

As they reached the third floor, Oscar baited his trap. "You can see the entire problem by looking through the window of this apartment." As he walked through the door and into the dimly lit room the chief uttered words he'd regret to his dying day: "Madam, may I inspect your shaft?" Naturally, his request had outraged the gay caballeros in the reception line. "Get on the end of the line and wait your turn, man!"

Chief McCarthy's outrage was stupendous. He verbally tore the hide from Lieutenant Anderson's back strip by strip. The idea that a member of his command would have the effrontery to set him up in such a manner appalled him. He was so annoyed that he wasn't thinking straight. Further investigation of the involved apartment would have revealed the fact that there was no window leading to any shaft.

Oscar lucked out as far as McCarthy and his departmental charges were concerned. But he failed to escape the wrath of Lieutenant Anderson. Never in the history of anyone assigned to Engine 58 had the lieutenant been more vitriolic. Later, in the company office, he had informed Oscar that he would be the recipient of some specialized treatment. "From the time you enter these quarters you will be productively occupied!"

Oscar scrubbed the latrines. Oscar shined the poles. Oscar serviced the apparatus, and Oscar picked up every 3:00 a.m. to 6:00 a.m. watch. The lieutenant's instructions to Billy Murray were specific: "If I find you picking up one of that clown's watches, your name will be mud!"

It's difficult to determine whether Oscar's subsequent adherence to protocol stemmed from the lieutenant's adamant attitude. Perhaps the moon was in a descendant position. Possibly the tide was low. In any event, he behaved himself awaiting the inevitable rising of the tide.

During this period of seeming normality there came a time when that man of infinite patience—Jack Whalen—retired. Whalen was a really fine human being who had served as aide to the klutz Chief McCarthy for many months. Subject to the despotic actions of McCarthy, and unable to swing a transfer, Whalen had finally decided to pack it in. Since he has a rather exalted opinion of himself, it was only natural that Chief McCarthy would feel there would be a rush of personnel only too anxious to take Whalen's place. After all, look at the opportunities. No house watch duty. No committee work. A crack at an excellent vacation pick every year. The opportunity to bask in the reflected glory of Chief McCarthy. Who could ask for anything more? *No one—absolutely no one.*

Annoyed that none of the battalion personnel had the good

sense to fight over the opportunity to drive him, Chief McCarthy sent out a circular asking for volunteers. Naturally, there was much speculation concerning the possibility of anyone stepping up for such an assignment. Since Pudgy Dunn had a good friend in the battalion, it was only natural that Lieutenant Anderson make inquiry concerning anyone stepping into the breach.

Pudgy's choice of verbiage had been descriptive and slightly puzzling. "There's one volunteer, lieutenant. The tide is high and the moon is full." The lieutenant wasn't in the mood for riddles and demanded a name. Pudgy gave it to him. "The name of the fish cake, Lieutenant, is OSCAR FUCKING RATNER."

It was rumored that Chief McCarthy had informed headquarters he'd rather drive himself than be subjected to Ratner's paranoia. In any event, one Nobert Finnigan of Ladder 14 was dragged out of obscurity and forced to act as aide to the local martinet.

Finnigan's threats to resign from the union, to quit the job, or to commit suicide were ignored. Gillian's comments concerning the matter may or may not have met with the approval of the majority of Harlem's firefighters: "Any guy with a handle like Nobert deserves no sympathy."

In a desperate effort to improve his status, Finnigan resorted to study. He enrolled in the Delehanty Institute and was seldom seen without study material of one sort or another. An active and vocal agnostic, he'd also resumed religion to the point of making a novena at St. Paul's, thus causing Captain Cullen to observe that even a bastard like Chief McCarthy was put on earth for some positive purpose. It was an attitude heartily agreed to by the members of the Harlem brigade.

The Chef

If there's a normal person, a truly normal human being assigned to these units, that man is John Silensa. Quietly efficient, a genuinely nice individual, he's the firehouse chef. Regarded by many as the outstanding culinary expert in the area—if not in the entire job—he devotes his non-firefighting activities to a variety of menus. Preparation and purchasing of food are basic parts of Silensa's department life. John's day seldom varies. Rain or shine, he's in the kitchen.

It's raining on this dismal Wednesday in early November and Silensa's mood matches the weather. Alone in the kitchen he stands in front of the oven debating whether or not to add raisins to his rice pudding. He's in a no-win situation and it concerns him deeply. "That fucking Gillian and his goddamned diet!" The pudding is ready to go and John has to make a decision. Henderson demands raisins and failure to provide that little extra will set him off on one of his tirades.

Silensa looks at the clock. It's 11:15 and time for a decision. The pudding has to go into the oven *now*. He's made up his mind. The hell with Gillian—let that big stiff pick out the raisins. Silensa adds an entire box of raisins and vigorously stirs them through the mixture before slamming the door. One crack concerning this particular meal and it'll be the last one he places on the kitchen table.

Again he looks at the clock. It's time to start on the meatloaf. He lights a cigarette and checks on his supplies. The ground beef, the eggs, the cans of tomato sauce and the parmesan cheese are all on hand. He's ready to go. He mixes the ingredients and silently debates the addition of a dash of oregano. Most of the guys are inclined to favor a little zest. Naturally, there are exceptions. Only last week Alcock had threatened to brown-bag it if garlic in any form was used. How a man can possibly prepare a meal without a touch of garlic escapes Silensa. The hell with Alcock. Let him stay out of the meals. A touch of garlic never harmed anyone.

Perhaps his wife is right. She's told him often enough, "Why knock yourself out for that pack of ingrates?" As he kneads the mixture, he's sure she's on target. Does anyone ever show any appreciation? Ever offer a compliment? A kind word? The hell they do. Most of them act as if he were some huge joke.

John considers the episode of the veal cutlets. Those rotten bastards. Six pounds of veal cutlets down the drain. He wasn't surprised that Woody Roberts, one of the retired men, had spent the night in the bunkroom. He was surprised that Woody had pissed the bed. Imagine a grown man tying on a load to that extent. It hadn't occurred to John that they'd used the flat iron to press out Woody's sodden pants. Of course, John had used that very iron to flatten out the cutlets. They wouldn't listen to reason. They'd ordered sandwiches from the deli. Twenty-two dollars worth of fucking cutlets up shit's creek. He should have resigned as company chef on the spot.

Silensa coughs as he draws deeply on his cigarette. "Gotta kick this habit before I really get hooked!" The fact that he's been a three-pack-a-day man for over twenty years escapes him. Silently he ponders the number of men to be fed and considers the possibility of stretching out the meatloaf by the addition of bread crumbs. He compromises by cracking two extra eggs into the mixture before placing it in the oven.

As he rinses his hands at the kitchen sink, Silensa prays there won't be a run prior to serving his meal. There's nothing more disturbing than putting an over-cooked meal on the table. Momentarily, he contemplates preparing some garlic bread but abandons the idea since Alcock's on duty. The hell with it. Arguing with that jerk simply isn't worth the effort.

He hopes he hasn't underestimated the quantity of food required to feed these apes. He's certain that cooking for this crew would qualify a man to figure out the menu for the Bronx Zoo. Silently he contemplates the capacities of the likes of Murray, Fitzmaurice and Gillian, wondering where the hell they put it all. Even that skinny bastard of a proby, Brennan, packs away food like it's going out of style. As he thinks of Brennan, he's made up his mind on one point. That hairy character will not weasel out of doing the dishes today. It's traditional for the junior man to clean up after a meal and John agrees with this wholeheartedly.

Silensa reaches into the cupboard for a supply of dinner plates and spreads them around the table. Taking a half a dozen loaves of Italian bread, he slices them rapidly and contemplates the variety of ploys Brennan had used to avoid contact with anything remotely associated with cleaning up the kitchen. There had been the legitimate injury to his hand requiring several stitches—an injury bandaged for some three weeks longer than necessary. Silensa was not amazed that a minor burn to the same hand had been covered by a Band-Aid for a considerable length of time. His current claim of an allergic reaction to soap powder and hot water was not unexpected.

A very satisfying aroma starts to fill the kitchen as the chef proceeds to the kitchen blackboard. He lists the names of the men in on the meal, totals the price of provisions and determines the cost of the meal. It's $2.15 per man. John figures this sum will set Gillian into a rage. Everything causes Gillian to shout at the top of his lungs.

John is sure of one thing. If Gillian shouts loud enough, he'll be requested to take up the duties of company chef. Silently John muses on the possibility of sitting down to a meal prepared by someone else. It's something he hasn't done for a long time. It's possible it might just be satisfying to criticize someone else's effort, to bitch about the price of food, to make asinine suggestions concerning the improvement of someone else's meal.

The chef is always amazed that some of these suggestions are absolutely out of this world. He considers Willie Burrell's ideas concerning soul food. He's utterly confused that soul food consists of something called chitterlings. Willie's explanation listing the item as hogs' innards disgusts him. Silensa finds beyond belief Gillian's statement that he's not only tried chitterlings but actually enjoyed them.

The variety of other bullshit suggestions concerning corned beef and cabbage, sauerbraten, boiled beef and horseradish sauce, and a host of other items allegedly prepared without parmesan cheese, garlic, tomato sauce and all the other magical ingredients required for a decent meal nauseate Silensa. "Them animals—what do they know about good food?"

It isn't only menu suggestions that bother Silensa. The smart-assed wisecracks are just as annoying. Tuna fish salad has to be described as cat food by Henderson. A serving of macaroni and cheese sauce isn't complete without Fitzmaurice gazing into the pot and making inquiry as to who puked. The heady, zesty aroma of parmesan cheese will require Pudgy Dunn to enquire as to who shit! John's resolve to pack the whole damned thing in is strengthened by the clamoring of these same characters for seconds. Let them get another patsy. First crack out of the box today and they get themselves a new chef.

A bell hits in, a close one. John breathes a sigh of relief. He's not in the mood for a fouled-up meal. He opens the oven door and gazes in at the meatloaf and rice pudding. Ten more minutes and he'll call the animals. Hopefully, Ratner will exhibit sufficient courtesy to have washed his hands after having worked on the pumper motor. If all goes well, someone might even offer a compliment. Failing that, this might be the one time no one utters a smart-ass remark. It might also be the occasion for thirty-two days in November.

The aromas have permeated the upper atmosphere and the crew is starting to head for the kitchen. Roger is the first to arrive, immediately followed by the new proby, Jack McBride. Brennan is making sure the big guy is properly indoctrinated. "It's the absolute obligation of the newest man to clean up the kitchen after every meal!" Now that he has a smidgen of seniority, Brennan will be saddling McBride with all the minor tasks he's been ducking for the past year and a half.

Fitzmaurice is next and he has the oven door open inspecting its contents. "Hey, John, someone puked in the oven!" Silensa doesn't have to turn around to identify the next arrival. The "Who shit?" of Pudgy Dunn is identification enough.

Henderson is sitting down buttering a piece of bread, sniffing the atmosphere like a bird dog. "I sincerely hope I am not about to be served Kennel Ration again!"

Gillian, hulking through the kitchen door, stops to check Silensa's figures on the black board. "Are you trying to bankrupt me? How the hell many times do I have to plead with you to keep down the cost of these meals?"

Ratner, fresh from his assault on the pumper motor, and totally alien regarding an application of soap and water, is demanding service. "C'mon, John, let's get the fuckin' show on the road. I'm starving!"

Burrell and Murray are out of the cellar sweating profusely from their karate endeavors. Burrell is breathing in deeply. "Sure don't smell like no soul food to me!" Murray is in complete agreement. "You're absolutely right, Willie. It's about time we had a feed of corned beef and cabbage!"

The officers are downstairs. The aromas had reached the office level and Captain Cullen and Lieutenant Anderson stand plate in hand waiting for John to ladle out a portion of meatloaf. Shortly, everyone is seated. For a while there's hardly a word. Finally the captain speaks. "John, you're the best goddamned cook in the New York City Fire Department."

Slowly Silensa rises from his seat and proceeds towards the calendar on the kitchen wall. The last time he'd looked there'd been thirty days listed for the month of November. Somehow, in some miraculous fashion, two extra days have been added. It's all very mysterious.

Pudgy's Brainstorm

Every firehouse enjoys at least one character. The fact that Engine 58 and Ladder 26 have more than their share of oddballs is somewhat distinctive. Any group of company officers commanding the likes of Gillian, Ratner, Murray and Fitzmaurice might be inclined to shout "Hold! Enough!"—and they'd be right. For the officers assigned to the Fire Factory, however, there's more. There's Pudgy Dunn.

If one were to compile a history of "Fire Department Characters," an entire chapter would have to be devoted to Pudgy Dunn. Pudgy is known to *every* man, in *every* unit throughout the job. Pudgy is an organizer. He simply gets things done. Family picnics, beach parties, softball games, annual dinner dances, promotion and retirement parties. You name it and Pudgy's in charge.

It would seem that a man devoting such time and energy to the general welfare would be honored. Such is not the case. If ever a man were reviled, abused, berated and generally put upon, Pudgy is that man. For all of this, he has an explanation. "Them bastards enjoy breaking my balls!" Truthfully, they love the man. Being perverse, they have a rather odd method of demonstrating their feelings.

There is seldom a week throughout the year when Pudgy is not burdened with preparations for one event or another. Some of these affairs overlap. A portion of his day at the family picnic may be spent figuring out the logistics associated with a forthcoming promotion or retirement party. Pudgy gains nothing from these activities other than the feeling of a job well done. The certainty that he'll be harassed for anything and everything associated with even the most minute of foul-ups is as sure as the rising sun:

"That table got more fuckin' hotdogs than we got!"
"Sam Morrissey's kid just beat the shit out of my son and I want to know what you're going to do about it?"
"Somebody goosed my wife while we were dancing!"
"How come none of these rackets are ever held on Staten Island?"

And so forth, and so forth, and so forth. The finale to these affairs is inevitable. Pudgy resigns. "Get yourselves another fuckin' patsy. I've had it!" The following week finds him coming up with plans for another event. Since Pudgy is an eccentric, some of these affairs are unique and none more bizarre than his current brainstorm. Pudgy has decided to form and coach a football team composed of fire department personnel. The team will challenge the police department with proceeds donated to a worthy charity.

If Pudgy has a middle name, it's persistence. No one sticks to an issue with such tenacity. The average person making a proposal concerning an event similar to Pudgy's "Fun City Bowl" would have folded his tents like the proverbial Arab on meeting such formidable opposition. Not Pudgy. Pudgy thrives on opposition. The original forms soliciting information from those interested came back with a variety of suggestions. Most of them questioned Pudgy's sanity. Pudgy was attacked on every front. Who would supply equipment? Where would the game be played? What arrangements would be made for practice sessions? Would the department grant leaves? Would members be protected in the event of injury? Amazingly, support for the game came from sources outside of both departments. Persons in the media approached the mayor's office suggesting the idea had merit. Naturally, once the mayor approved of the project the upper echelons of both departments leaped in claiming credit for Pudgy's idea.

Forming a coaching staff would be no problem. Any number of firefighters run Pop Warner, and other sandlot teams and some members are on the coaching staffs of local high schools. A supporting staff consisting of a trainer, an equipment manager and a person to guard valuables would have to be recruited. Pudgy has one fear insofar as recruiting assistance is concerned, and that is how to sell Billy Murray the idea of playing without becoming involved with Billy's father. Billy Murray is a class athlete with a host of collegiate and semi-professional experience. Old man Murray, in Pudgy's considered opinion, is a pain in the ass. The deepening feud between the pair shows no sign of abatement.

The meeting of prospective personnel was held in the Knights of Columbus building in the Nostrand Avenue section of Brooklyn. It set the trend insofar as attitudes were concerned. Gillian got lost. He always gets lost in Brooklyn. Gillian despises Brooklyn and everything associated with the borough. "This place is the pits. I refuse to be associated with an organization so devoid of class that they hold meetings in fucking Brooklyn." Placating Gillian will be a must. The guy's professional football experience makes him vital to Pudgy's plans.

One of Pudgy's weaknesses is his reluctance to delegate authority. His insistence on staying close to every phase of each project gets him into trouble. This football game will be no different. Since a large portion of game revenue will be derived from the sale of refreshments, contacts must be made with suppliers. Pudgy's decision to order beer from the Schaeffer Brewing Company gives retired Lieutenant Murray an opening. The lieutenant is all over Pudgy accusing him of being anti-New York City. Since Schaeffer has moved its base of operations from the city and cost the area thousands of jobs, he has a point. And so has Pudgy. "There are no longer any fucking breweries in New York City. What the hell difference does it make who I order from?" Murray has an answer to *that* problem. "Alcohol rots the brain. It turns men into absolute assholes. Look what it's done to you!"

Practice sessions are chaotic. The members are required to participate on their off-time and leaves will not be granted. Cooperation, insofar as mutual exchanges of tours, is as far as the department will go. There will be a scheduled practice when there are two quarterbacks and no center. The following session will find all defensive personnel present with three quarters of the offensive team missing. The contrast in football experience among the various members is appalling. Gillian, Murray, McBride, Fitzmaurice and seven or eight other members have fabulous football backgrounds, while others hardly know one end of the ball from the other. There came a time when Pudgy, desperate to get an offensive workout going, asked for volunteers for the position of center. The regular center, an excellent ballplayer, was absent. A huge character named Arthur Durken stepped up and it was soon apparent that this guy had never played football. Bending over, he kept hitting himself in the rump with the ball instead of handing it to the quarterback. Pudgy was amazed. "Why do you keep trying to shove that ball up your ass?"

A man of lesser courage would have packed the entire thing in after a couple of sessions. For all his faults, Pudgy Dunn has never learned the meaning of the word quit. The ball game was scheduled. The ball game would be played. If practice sessions weren't working out, perhaps the answer might lie in a practice game. Accordingly, Pudgy scheduled a game with a group of long-term convicts incarcerated in a maximum security prison about one hundred miles north of New York City. Surely there would be no problem. Hire a bus, provide some beer for the return trip, play a fun game with the convicts and work out a few of the kinks.

Trouble, as usual, started with Gillian. Throughout his career he'd used the number 69. Old Man Murray—just as thick as Pudgy or Gillian—had handed out uniform 69 to another character. Gillian brooded over the matter for some ten days and finally came to a decision. He picked up the phone in his Westchester County home and dialed Western Union. The resultant telegram delivered to Pudgy's Brooklyn home was terse and to the point. "Refuse to compete unless issued number 69 STOP Will not associate with a team scheduling games in the Borough of Brooklyn STOP." Pudgy was outraged. "That telegram from Western Fucking Union almost gave me a heart attack. Any other telegrams I ever got, someone died!" The matter of the number was solved by Larry Fitzmaurice. Approaching the inept Arthur Durken, he'd asked him politely to exchange numbers with Gillian and on Arthur's refusal, Larry had threatened to "punch the shit out of Durken." The exchange of jerseys took place some five minutes later.

Since nothing in the world of Pudgy Dunn runs smoothly, the bus scheduled to take the players to the practice game lacked restroom facilities. This shortcoming was corrected by the purchase of a large funnel and a short length of garden hose. When in use the hose would be held out of a window with the variety of firefighters utilizing the funnel as a urinal. It was John Dale of Engine 230 who pointed out the contraption's obvious shortcomings. "It'll work out fine until a guy has to move his bowels!"

The point of departure selected was The Mariners Inn on Avenue S in Brooklyn. Gillian and a few of the upstaters would meet the others at the prison. Naturally, Pudgy had forbidden the consumption of any alcoholic beverages prior to game time, and of course the guys hadn't paid him the slightest attention. Lieutenant Murray had an opinion on the matter. "Anyone stupid enough to have a bunch of firemen meet in front of a gin mill deserves what he gets!"

To make sure all were accounted for, Pudgy had counted heads as each man entered. As the firemen boarded, they proceeded out of the rear exit and lined up again. When the count reached 104, Pudgy decided to hell with it and told the driver to start the bus.

Due to a variety of circumstances the bus was late in starting and Pudgy had decided to save time by having the trainer tape the personnel en route. Normally, the plan had merit. Selecting Brian Fogarty as trainer had been an excellent idea. Not only is the man an EMT, he's also a registered nurse. On this particular day he was also intoxicated. The lengthy layover at The Mariners Inn had taken its toll on Fogarty, and some of the playing personnel were in similar shape. There were those who had double doses of tape on their left ankle with no tape on their right. One man found himself secured to a portion of the bus, and the vast majority of the fire department athletes arrived untaped.

Despite Pudgy's resistance, beer had been smuggled aboard

and half of his personnel are well on the way to being basket cases. Cigarette smoke hangs over the length of the bus and the conduct of the prospective athletes is outrageous. Fitzmaurice argues loudly with Murray over the merits of karate as opposed to old-fashioned brawling. A passing Volkswagon, windows open, was inundated with a flow of urine escaping from the improvised latrine. Pudgy was close to becoming a mental case. Not only was this day developing into a fiasco, but retired Lieutenant Murray was driving him to distraction. "Some lieutenant you'll make. You couldn't control a boy scout troop. They'll keep half of these clowns in that jail! I only hope they keep you, too!"

Actually, the practice game didn't turn out all that badly. Since some of the firefighters were in their cups, the convicts built up a half time lead of 12-0. Tom Dorning, an excellent running back with collegiate experience, had two touchdowns called back. On each occasion Arthur Durken had clipped an opponent some twenty yards in back of the speeding Dorning. On the second occasion Pudgy had clipped Durken with a water bucket.

Whether Pudgy's impassioned half time oratory had any affects is debatable. Lieutenant Murray's contention that "these bums have sweated out all that beer" had merit. Whatever the reason, the fire department's offensive line sparked by Gillian, Fitzmaurice, Murray, McBride and Dale tore holes in the prison defense. Dorning scored three times, icing the game. Beating an inept prison eleven by one score wasn't much of an accomplishment. The police department's excellent team would be a whole other ball game.

Word has passed around concerning the respective conditions of the teams competing in the Fun City Bowl. The cops are in excellent shape. They are comprised of a large squad of experienced athletes and they are handled by a no-nonsense coach. All men interested in playing are assigned to the 4:00 p.m. to midnight shift. Since the police department prefers as many personnel as possible working during this troublesome period, things work out beautifully. Practice sessions are well attended. In comparison to the fire department's Keystone

Comedy practice, the cops go at things hammer and tongs. If you fail to show for practice without a valid excuse, you are gone. The police had scouted the prison practice game and developed a strategy. By sheer coincidence the starting lineup of the fire department is far superior to their opponents. Dorning, Murray, Gillian, McBride, Dale and Jennings, the fantastically gifted black split end, and five or six others could start on any college team in the country. There's a weakness, however, and it's no secret. It's expressed succinctly by Pudgy. "This team is one fucking deep at every position. Those cops will make every effort to wear us down!" Pudgy is right. That will be the cops' strategy. Keep on throwing in fresh troops, they reason, and Pudgy will have to remove some of his magnificent starting members and throw in the clowns.

Pudgy expected trouble with Gillian over the game site. Midwood High School Field had been selected and Midwood High School is in Brooklyn. At this stage the contest could take place in Nome, Alaska as far as Gillian is concerned. His brother-in-law will be playing on the PD squad and has publicly announced he will flatten that phony bastard Gillian in the center of Midwood Field. Gillian has a few plans of his own. "If that numbskull Conway had a brain, I'd perform a lobotomy on him. Next Saturday night I'll just settle for beating the shit out of him!"

The game's a sellout. Both teams will donate all the proceeds to various orphan and widows' funds within their respective jobs. It's an election year and naturally all the politically motivated will be present. Pudgy's final workouts are interrupted by a variety of interviews and picture taking sessions. Every hack running for office is making political hay out of the game. To make matters worse, Lieutenant Murray is still breaking his chops. "Install the Notre Dame shift, you asshole. It's our only hope." It makes little difference that Lieutenant Murray couldn't distinguish the Notre Dame sweep from a telegraph pole. He's having a magnificent time driving his enemy up the wall. He's also an excellent equipment manager and there's no way Pudgy can get rid of him.

The clear, beautiful, Saturday night selected for the game

has arrived. The lights are on and the astro-turfed playing surface is in perfect shape. The stadium is filled to capacity and refreshment stands, particularly those selling beer, are doing a land-office business. The fire department locker room is quiet. They realize they're in for a rough night. Pudgy paces the area between lockers. Gillian, Fitzmaurice, Jenkins and the starting quarterback Bernardi have yet to put in an appearance. Pudgy looks at his watch. "Where are those fucking numbskulls?" There are other problems. McBride has left his football cleats at home and will have to make a fast trip to retrieve them. Lieutenant Murray has secured a huge supply of gum and a bushel of oranges and is demanding payment. Gillian has arrived. As usual, he'd been lost. He'd also been gifted with a traffic ticket. "That fucking ticket gets paid by the fire department or number 69 sits this game out!"

This small band of fire department football players is complete at last. Gillian's been placated. His ticket will be paid by the organization. Lieutenant Murray is heartbroken. Pudgy'd paid for the oranges and gum without comment. The possibility of driving Pudgy clear around the bend over the items had seemed so certain. Murray will have to dream up another ploy.

Pudgy's football strategy is simple. Recognizing the fabulous talents associated with Dorning, he realizes the entire police defense will be geared towards stopping this man. Pudgy's installed an end-around-run that will hopefully utilize the blinding speed of Jenkins. If the police spend enough time concentrating on Dorning, it just might work. The fourth quarter will be Pudgy's travail. His small squad will be exhausted by that time. Scoring early and often, then holding on, seems the only hope.

They're lined up, ready to move out. Fitzmaurice is the team captain and will lead the charge down the runway and out on to the field. The referees have called for the teams. It's time to go—time to face up to a few realities—time to wish they'd taken the practice sessions a bit more seriously.

The fire department's won the toss and the special teams are lined up awaiting the referee's whistle. Clancy, the cops' excellent kicker, booms one down to the five-yard line. Jenkins flies down the middle, staying inside the wedge. Behind some excellent blocking he cuts to his left heading for the sidelines. He's off and running, finally being shoved out of bounds on the P.D. five-yard line. It's all a waste of time. Once again, Arthur Durken's thrown a clip yards behind the point of action. The flag on the twenty moves the ball back to the fire department's ten-yard line.

Pudgy is giving a marvelous imitation of a man applying for admission to one of the state's mental institutions. Screaming at Durken, questioning the guy's legitimacy, he makes a promise to cut his own throat prior to reinserting the man for as much as one play. Bernardi calls the first play. "Fake right, dive left on two." Dorning carrying the ball is good for two yards and no more. The cops are watching his every move. With Dorning plowing up the middle for four, Bernardi figures it's as good a time as any to try Pudgy's end-around-run. It works like a charm. Dorning, running left, flips the ball to Jenkins who's off and running behind an awesome wall furnished by Gillian, Murray, Fitzmaurice and McBride. It's good for seventy-five yards and a touchdown. The uproar inside Midwood is fantastic. The sound must be audible as far south as Kings Highway. The touchdown had little meaning to Gillian. He'd cut down his brother-in-law. He laid the guy out like a rug. As he lines up for the extra point, he shouts in Conway's direction. "Hey, asshole! Remember what that guy said in the football scene in the movie MASH? Next play, off goes your fucking head!"

On the first series run by the police department a trend is set. Fresh personnel are being run in on every play. The fire department gives three first downs before forcing their opponents to kick. During the series they'd lost their excellent defensive tackle Mike LeHane for the balance of the game. Clancy's kick goes out of bounds on the four, leaving Pudgy's crew in a hole. Looking sharp, Dorning runs for two first downs before Bernardi tries the end-around again. Jenkins is thrown for a three-yard loss. The next set of downs finds the fire department holding inside the ten. Kenny McPherson, an excellent defensive end for the fire department, is carried off the field.

The second quarter finds the cops in possession of the ball for a full eleven minutes. The fire department squad is close to exhaustion. Attempting to score before the half, the police had tried a pass with disastrous results. Joe Hennessey, at cornerback, had picked one off and run it back for the fire department's second score. As the teams come off the field at the end of the half, it's hard to rationalize the fire department's fourteen-point lead. The cops look fresh as daisies. Seven starting ballplayers are out of action for the fire department. The cops have competent personnel they haven't even had the opportunity to use. The second half will be rough for the firefighters—very rough.

The gloom in the fire department dressing room is thick enough to slice. They have the look of a beaten team. Heads pick up on a report concerning half-time activity on the field. During a performance by the police department piper band, the field had been streaked by Roger Brennan and Kevin O'Hare, another mad firefighter from Harlem. The pair, stark naked, bearing a banner "Beat The Cops!" had outraged the brass. The Fire Commissioner had demanded the capture of the offenders. The streakers had escaped scot-free. Pudgy hopes he'll be as fortunate.

Still looking for a way of torturing Pudgy, Lieutenant Murray had approached his enemy. "About these oranges. Do you want them halved, quartered or squeezed?" It was all Pudgy needed. "What am I? A Needick's fucking stand operator? Get off my goddamned back!" Paradoxically, the exchange resulted in a revival of outlook on the part of the team. Physically and emotionally upset, Pudgy had headed for the urinal where he proceeded to vomit. In a normal society an incident of this sort would certainly evoke sympathy. There's little that's normal about the fire department. Standing en masse the ball club shouted. "Puke, Pudgy, Puke! Puke, Pudgy, Puke!" Running out on the ballfield they're still shrieking the same asinine war cry. It's fine with Pudgy. "If it revives those crazy bastards, I'll even kiss that miserable old goat Murray!"

They aren't revived for long. From the opening kickoff the third quarter sees the police department in complete control. No finesse. Nothing spectacular. Straight up the middle for five, six or seven yards a carry. Pudgy's only consolation is time. The police strategy is eating up the clock. Burned by that one interception, and emboldened by the success of their dogged running game, they stick to a successful formula. They scored at 11:04 of the third period.

By the middle of the fourth quarter, Pudgy is reduced to going both ways with Gillian, Fitzmaurice, McBride and Billy Murray. Using these men on both offense and defense will be exhausting. With four minutes to go, this bruised and battered quartet, sparking the middle of the fire department defense, had grudgingly surrendered the tying touchdown. Briefly, fire department hopes had revived on a thirty-yard gainer by Dorning. A fumble on the next play surrendered the ball to a surging police department offense. It looked like it was all over but the shouting.

Smashing ahead for three consecutive first downs, the police department brought the ball inside the firefighters' ten. Inside the fire department defensive huddle, Larry Fitzmaurice says a silent prayer. "Give us a break on this one, Lord, and I can die happy. I'll never ask another favor!"

Larry had been amazed at the turn of events. Pudgy later described the action as something right out of a "Hollywood fucking movie!" Filling in at middle line backer, Billy Murray had guessed right. Blitzing the number two hole, he'd smashed the ball carrier at the line of scrimmage, forcing him to cough up the ball. Larry plucked the pigskin out of the air and was gone. Remarkably fast for a man of his build, there is no catching old number 62. It's all over. Strangely, Pudgy isn't happy at all. Once again, he'd been zapped by his old enemy. Lieutenant Murray had talked the fire department squad into awarding the game ball to Arthur Durken.

While Pudgy ground his teeth, Arthur had spent an inordinately long time getting his teammates to autograph the ball. He was smart enough not to approach Pudgy. While not much of a football player, Arthur's no dummy—no dummy at all.

Bernie Schwartz

People attain notoriety in a variety of ways. Some achieve fame due to their own efforts, and others have it thrust upon them. Bernie Schwartz is such a person. Certainly, as a middle-aged man he'd hardly request a transfer to Harlem. Still, here he is heading north from Brooklyn, towards Engine 58, mumbling to himself concerning life's vicissitudes.

Bernie doesn't have to turn his car radio on to be informed of conditions on the northbound section of the FDR Drive. As far as the eye can see, bumper to bumper traffic inches torturously ahead. The pace gives him time to think, to consider his wife's demands about packing in the job and to mull over the advice of his friend Chief McManus. "Bernie! What's a nice Jewish boy like you doing in a Harlem firehouse?"

They're concerned for him—McManus and his wife—both terribly worried abut a forty-seven year old man reporting for duty in one of the busiest firehouses on the face of the earth. There had been a time when Bernie, his wife, Chief McManus or anyone else, for that matter, wouldn't have given a second thought regarding Schwartz's assignment. That, however, had been long ago. Bernie's seventeen-year experience in the Brownsville section of Brooklyn is a thing of the past.

For the five years he'd been a part of the Sheepshead Bay unit, Bernie performed the functions required of a man in that area. The neighborhood was a soft touch and he regarded that as his due. Seventeen years of horrendous fire duty, seventeen years of taking his lumps in one of the busiest areas in town had earned him a respite. Like they say in Flatbush —He's entitled.

The traffic opens up briefly and Bernie whips over to the right-hand lane. Ahead he can spot the flashing lights of a squad car. There's an accident in the left-hand lane. Bernie hopes he can make the 6:00 p.m. roll call. He wouldn't want to be late for his first tour. Not that it makes a hell of a lot of difference when a man has twenty-two years in the job.

The twenty-two years are what's driving his wife to distraction. He's sure of that. She wants him to retire. She can't understand his refusal to be driven out of the job. Neither can Chief McManus.

It's a matter of principle as far as Bernie is concerned. Somehow he'll manage to survive. Bernie considers himself one of the all-time great survivors.

He'd received the notice from headquarters ordering him to report for questioning concerning a confidential matter and he'd been puzzled. What could confidentiality and Bernie Schwartz have in common? He soon found out.

Along with many of his peers, Bernie moonlights. The utter impossibility of meeting his obligations on his fire department income is readily apparent. It's the manner in which Bernie moonlights that sets him apart. While his fellow firefighters stack grocery shelves, tend bar, paint apartments, drive taxis, act as bouncers, serve as ushers, sell their services in the myriad part-time job market servicing New York City, Bernie runs his own insurance business.

This part-time occupation enables him to live like a Deputy Chief of Department while sending a son through dental school but has never interfered with the excellent relationship Bernie enjoys with his friends throughout the job. Actually, the bulk of his clients are firefighters and therein lies Bernie's problems with the brass.

He'd cooled his heels outside of the office of one of the Deputy Fire Commissioners for four hours last Thursday and got hotter under the collar as time went on. His humor hardly improved on admittance to this character's office. Briefly, this political hack had demanded a total list of each and every department customer of Bernie's. The list was to include names, addresses, company units and the amount and type of each and every policy carried by the Schwartz Agency.

Bernie told the guy to kiss his ass. The privacy of the broker-client relationship would not be violated. The threat of a transfer to Harlem had followed. It hadn't surprised Bernie to learn that the Deputy Commissioner had been dumbfounded at his refusal. The man's further statement that Schwartz would either cave in or put in his retirement paper had firmed Schwartz's intention of staying at Engine 58 for a minimum of one year prior to any thought of retirement. Schwartz is adamant on this point. No chicken shit politician is driving Bernie Schwartz out of the job. No way.

He's reached the U.N. building and the traffic is speeding up. The extra lane opened up as they pass the accident and this enables Bernie's Cadillac to pick up speed. The Caddie's the thing on his mind for the moment. Leaving a new Caddie outside of a Harlem firehouse isn't too bright. It's hardly a thing he'd recommend to one of his customers. Perhaps he'll pick up a secondhand car for the ride from Flatbush.

Bernie whips off the Drive at 96th Street and heads north on First Avenue. He's got a shot at making the 6:00 p.m. roll call. He wonders if Oscar Ratner is still assigned to Engine 58. He'd been appointed with that crazy bastard. Oscar had been in one lunatic episode after another in probationary school.

Bernie turns left on 115th Street tooling the Caddie over towards Fifth Avenue. He notes that the general condition of the area looks worse than Brownsville. He turns left on Fifth.

The only available parking space is further from the firehouse than he'd like. He'll have to keep his eyes peeled for a closer spot. He locks the car and opens the trunk. As he digs out his rubber coat, boots and helmet, several of the locals look at him in amazement. Their difficulty in rationalizing a firefighter with a brand new Cadillac is similar to the Deputy Commissioner's. Bernie is contented that at least they weren't demanding a list of his clients.

It's two weeks since Bernie's transfer. Two weeks of misery. Bernie now realizes he's middle-aged. The fact has been indelibly impressed on him by three all-hands fires, a fourth alarm, a host of minor runs and a myriad of false alarms. He'd forgotten what a busy house was all about. Seventeen runs on Friday. Nineteen runs on Saturday. His head aches and he's found out about muscles he hadn't known he possessed. One of the chiefs is an absolute bastard—a stiff named McCarthy

Perhaps his wife is right. Maybe it's all too much for a man so far out of touch. On the brighter side there's a couple of pluses. This guy Silensa is a master chef. Billy Murray picks up the late watches for study purposes. The bosses on Bernie's platoon are reasonable men. They realize he's doing his best. They offer nothing but encouragement. He'll try to stick it out on general principle. He'll try to put in that year before he packs it in. It's going to be rough. Very rough.

Bernie's been here a month now. He drives a used Pontiac. He'd learned the hard way that new Cadillacs are best left out of Harlem. A smashed rear-view mirror and a missing aerial had been the convincers.

The aches and pains are disappearing. He's ten pounds lighter. His paunch is hardening up to a smooth middle. He takes his turn on the nozzle. For the first week or two he felt so out of touch he feared going near the thing. Not any more. He's a fireman once again. He has a purpose for fire department existence. Bernie Schwartz loves this job. Sure, the money from the agency really pays the bills. There's no doubt about that. The agency's simply a necessity, however, something he's not really wild about.

He's becoming one of the boys. He'd been screwed by that hairy bastard Brennan. That innocent looking choirboy had altered the watch list causing Schwartz to pick up an extra watch. Bernie will watch that character very carefully in future. The fact that Oscar Ratner had nicked him for a fast twenty that Bernie felt would never be repaid marked him a member of the fraternity victimized by the profligate Oscar.

Bernie's gone fishing with Gillian and has been asked to go hunting with Silensa. Captain Cullen has sought his advice concerning an insurance problem. Things are looking up. Really looking up.

He's been here for two months. The word motherfucker no longer bothers him. The very expression made his skin crawl prior to his first pay check at Engine 58. It's just verbiage now, part of the local vocabulary. He's been reamed by that bastard Chief McCarthy. Three extra late watches for being caught in the kitchen while assigned to house watch duty. The monumental tongue-lashing thrown in with the extra watches has made him a part of a far from select group. Everyone in Harlem hates McCarthy.

It's three months later. Bernie is seriously thinking of making Chief McCarthy a partner in his insurance brokerage. Obviously in communication with headquarters, McCarthy has spoken at length in every local firehouse concerning the inadvisability of transacting business with the Schwartz Agency.

It was magical. One word from that stiff McCarthy and members of the various Harlem units are swinging business Bernie's way. Actually, word had been passed around the job concerning Bernie's gutsy performance with the Deputy Commissioner. Firefighters are very perverse individuals. The fact that headquarters saw fit to shaft Bernie only made his agency more desirable. Business has increased to such an extent it was necessary to hire another girl. Bernie is thinking of ordering new stationery. The Schwartz, McCarthy Agency has a certain ring to it.

Bernie's on medical leave. A back draft had blown Schwartz, Murray and Lieutenant Anderson down a flight of stairs. Miraculously injuries were minor. Murray's left ear is singed. He has no eyebrows. The lieutenant sprained an ankle. Bernie has second degree burns on his left hand. It comes as no surprise that Chief McCarthy is recommending charges. Bernie had forgotten about his work gloves. He'd left them in one of his pockets.

Chief McManus has been successful in squashing the charges against Bernie. His pleas to Bernie to "Wake up and smell the coffee" are another matter.

Bernie is adamant. "I will not retire from the department. Not now. Not next year. Not five years from now. I like this job. It makes me feel useful. I'm going to be here at Engine 58 for a long time. A very long time."

The One Liner

Bernie Schwartz and the members assigned to these Harlem units realize that the big fire is the one that rates the ink in the local press. Every department member's aware of that fact. They also realize it's the mundane, everyday, smallish type fire, that occupies most of their time. These are the alarms that drag them endlessly out of quarters hour after hour after endless hour.

Statistically the average working fire requires no more than one hose line and for that the Harlem firefighter is eternally grateful. Stretching hose is tough, backbreaking work. It's something they can do without. There's little glamour in the one line fire. It seldom rates a headline. Nevertheless, it's there, consuming a large part of the firefighters' time and effort. Like small skirmishes taking place in a huge theater of war, the unpublished one line fire takes its toll. Many injuries and some of the deaths are attributed to these small fires. Some of the one line jobs are, of course, contained because there is a citizenry sufficiently intelligent to call for help. Other minor blazes are held in check because of the professionalism of the responding forces.

It's a nasty cold night and the men standing in the basement of the tenement just off Fifth Avenue and East 111th Street are annoyed. They feel Captain Cullen is overdoing things. He's Acting Battalion Chief tonight and he's replacing the vacationing Chief McCarthy. The one line stretched by Engine 58 had been used to extinguish the pile of rubbish up against the basement wall. Silensa, in particular, is steaming. The huge cauldron of spaghetti will be garbage by the time they're finished. Twenty minutes of standing around while the captain probed and pried; twenty minutes that could have been devoted to salvaging a meal.

None of the men are happy. Hanging around a rat infested basement is hardly their idea of fun. The dingy rubbish laden area is depressing. The variety of smells is best left to the imagination. Some of the comments have been rebellious. Henderson has been particularly vociferous. "What the fuck is he hanging around for? Next, he'll have us whitewashing the walls!"

Even Lieutenant Anderson's beginning to be concerned about the delay. Naturally, he hasn't voiced any comments in the presence of the men. Still, he regards it as odd that the captain should keep them milling around. He begins to wonder about the man's whereabouts. The lieutenant is beginning to become concerned because the captain and Pudgy Dunn had left for the upper reaches of the building some time ago.

Anderson had just about decided to send out a search party when Pudgy returned. "The captain wants the line upstairs!" The stretch, out of the basement and up into the first floor area, hadn't taken long. Nevertheless, it was sufficient for the members to let off steam. Gillian was outraged. "There must be something about that rank that turns a nice captain into a replica of that prick McCarthy!"

The entry into the smelly hallway and into one of the dingy first floor apartments was not without incident. The captain's order to open up a portion of the wall met with opposition. "Man, this here's my apartment. Ain't nobody gonna make any motherfucking holes in my walls!"

The holes were made and the small readily apparent nest of fire travelling up the inner recesses of the wall was quite evident. It was sufficiently noticeable to cause a few red faces. Gillian, Silensa, Henderson and a few others wouldn't be reading headlines concerning persons burned out of their homes—or worse. Nor would there be investigations regarding the rekindling of fires. An entry in the fire record journal would suffice: "One line stretched by the members of Engine 58. Fire extinguished with 20 gallons of water. Necessary ventilation and overhauling performed by members of Ladder

26."

There were no rescues. No heroics. No headlines. Just the loss of five pounds of spaghetti.

The alarm for the fire in the candy store on St. Nicholas Avenue and 112th Street was transmitted at 9:45 p.m. The pushing and shoving of the disorderly crowd in front of the store had impeded stretching the one line Lieutenant Anderson has deemed necessary for handling the situation. Through the glass panel of the door a small body of fire situated in the rear of the store can be seen growing in intensity. Sufficient heat has been generated to change the nature of the glass servicing the show window and the door itself. The glass is no longer transparent. It's now translucent. Dingily yellowish in appearance, it's lost its commercial value and will have to be replaced. The door is protected by a valuable commercial lock. The lock will be unaffected by any heat generated by this particular fire.

The store is closed for the day. A small sign indicating the owner's phone number is visible. Captain Cullen, commanding the firefighters assigned to Ladder 26, has a choice. He can order his subordinates to force the door using the variety of tools at their disposal and destroying the lock in the process. Sending for the owner and his keys, is Cullen's alternative. The possibility of the fire reaching major proportions while awaiting the owner's arrival must be dealt with. Being a professional, Cullen is aware of his responsibilities. The glass is now useless but the lock has value. Cullen orders his men to break the glass panel portion of the door and he reaches in and opens the lock manually.

As the engine company members stretch-in to handle this one line job, the displeasure of the crowd is evident. "Them motherfuckers really enjoy destroying someone else's property." To make matters more interesting, the owner has arrived and is aghast at the destructive actions of the firefighters. Attempts to explain the situation are useless. In this man's opinion, the actions of the firefighters are disgraceful. Heads will roll, as far as he's concerned. Phone calls will be made and vengeance extracted.

The form of vengeance attempted by the candy store owner

is old hat to these firefighters. The arriving fire marshall, called to investigate the claim of missing merchandise and a fairly large amount of cash, has been over this route before. He has a job to do and he has to be impartial. The owner's rationale is understandable when his biased mentality is considered. Why not make a little profit along with his vengeance? After all, no one will be hurt, other than the insurance company and the firefighters. The insurance company has plenty of money. The firemen? Fuck the firemen. Look what they've done to the store.

The marshall's request for a personal search of all firefighters present meets with one strenuous objection. Bernie Schwartz insists upon being placed under arrest prior to search. His further statements promising certain lawsuit in the event of false arrest slows down the wrath of the storekeeper. Bernie's expertise as an insurance broker ends the matter. Bernie volunteers the information that cash could not be covered by the owner's insurance policy. This bit of information further calms the owner. This one line fire has added a fund of knowledge as far as this local merchant is concerned. He's now also aware that heated glass, becoming translucent, loses its value. While not profitable, it will be something to discuss on a long winter's night.

The snow had reached a total of nine inches and the units have been in and out all tour. Engine 58 has responded to a special call for a fire in a panel truck at Lenox Avenue and 118th Street and the members realize they can handle the job with one line. Their immediate problem would be locating a hydrant. Once again the Sanitation Department has done a wonderful job of concealment. Every hydrant is buried in snow. As the truck burns with increasing intensity, the members dig in all directions trying to uncover a hydrant.

The actions of the firefighters are perplexing to at least one local resident. "Man, dig them crazy firemen. The man's motherfucker truck is burning to the ground and they shovelin' snow!"

Few people are about on this bitterly cold morning. Those with a bed to sleep in have the blankets tucked under their chins. The members of Engine 58 are out. They have little choice in the matter. The alarm transmitted at 3:50 a.m. for the huge tractor-trailer parked at Third Avenue and 119th Street had been handled by Engine 35. The members of Engine 58 are returning to quarters and proceeding along 116th Street. They have one thought in mind and that is getting the hell out of this piercing cold.

Ignatius Gonzales considers himself to be a proud man, a person demanding respect. For the eight months he'd lived with Felicita Morales in common-law relationship, he'd treated her with love and tenderness. He regarded her constant complaints about infidelity as ridiculous. A man must be a man. Ignatius regards multiple feminine relationships as essential to his image. Her complaints were outrageous and not to be tolerated. More important, her decision to take up with that clown Jose Martinez would have to be avenged. No one cuckolds Ignatius without paying the price. No one.

He had no problem obtaining five gallons of gasoline in a battered portable container. Adding an extra dollar to the purchase price had convinced the kid handling the pump that Ignatius was an all-right guy. Of course, it had been necessary to bolster his courage at the Bar of the Three Palms on Park Avenue. He will now seek his revenge as he staggers along 116th Street towards Felicita's new residence.

Moving stealthily into the tenement hallway, he'd sloshed gasoline around the floor. Discarding the empty can, Ignatius reaches into a pocket for a matchbook. Striking a match, he contemplates the sweetness of revenge. He has no thoughts concerning the eighteen other families sleeping in the tenement.

Gonzales has struck his match with disastrous effects. The hallway is on fire and so is Gonzales. His lack of knowledge concerning arson, his intoxication, and the porous can which has liberally soaked his clothing with gasoline have turned him into a torch. Screaming in agony, he races into the street.

Even the most blase of Harlem firefighters would have to be affected by the spectacle of a human torch speeding from a flaming hallway. The potential for disaster was, of course, evident. Only the immediate presence of Engine 58 enabled the fire to be handled by one line. The rapid stretching of hose and the prompt dousing of flames undoubtedly saved the occupants from disaster. Strangely, the presence of Engine 58 was helpful to Gonzales himself. The flames were smothered when Gonzales was wrapped in a spare turnout coat. Calling an ambulance via radio and insisting that the victim be transported to the Burn Center at the New York Hospital-Cornell Medical Center undoubtedly saved the idiot's life. What action the authorities will take when the man is eventually released is naturally problematic. After all, circumstances must be considered. He's genuinely sorry and no real damage was done. A few scorched doorways, some damage to the stairs and a few smoked up apartments are nothing in comparison to the damage prison might have on a man's psyche. Gonzales *did* say he was sorry. That should count for something. Considering the mentality of many local judges, Ignatius would probably do alright. He had suffered; burns are very painful; he was contrite. That should count for something.

Normally, Lieutenant Anderson finds Larry Fitzmaurice a pleasure to work with. The man's an excellent firefighter. He's sturdy, solid and dependable. Fitzie is also a barrel of laughs. Naturally, being human, Larry has one drawback. Impelled by the excitement of emergency conditions Larry will, on occasion, issue orders. Since there's only one person in charge of a unit, contradictory orders can be annoying and even dangerous. Of course, the lieutenant has brought the matter up. He's broached it repeatedly, as a matter of fact. "Keep your fucking mouth shut at fires!" Still Larry persists in forgetting himself. He never seems to learn. "Pass the goddamned lieutenant's test and then you can give all the orders you want!"

It was a muggy afternoon and Engine 58 had been special-called concerning a refrigerant leak in an apartment building on Seventh Avenue near 114th Street. Since there had been a trace of smoke associated with the refrigerator, a line had been stretched as a precautionary measure. Surprisingly, the machine was charged with sulphur dioxide, a refrigerant the lieutenant hadn't come up against for some time. Years back thousands of these boxes had plagued the Harlem area. As a refrigerant, the substance leaves little to be desired. It does its job. Once the gas lines spring a leak it can be a murderous situation. The noxious fumes can be deadly. The acrid, breathtaking odors have to be experienced to be believed.

Since he'd handled any number of these devices in the past, the lieutenant knew precisely how to proceed. Masks would be issued to all personnel. The special ropes carried for the purpose of moving similar devices would be brought to the involved apartment. Once the box had been removed to the street level, the refrigerant lines would be purged rendering the device harmless. As a finale, the lieutenant would order the refrigerator door removed. Too many small children had suffocated playing hide-and-seek in similarly abandoned devices.

So much for the best laid plans of mice and men. Fitzmaurice, Schwartz, Murray and McBride all masked and struggling with the bulky refrigerator had reached a point on the stairway midway between the second and third floors. The equally masked Anderson was in a position immediately below his men lending encouragement. Into this scene of activity there shortly came a voice issuing an order. "Take off the masks! We don't need them!" To his utter embarrassment Lieutenant Anderson removed his face piece along with the rest of the men. Since he was the only officer present, he should have realized Fitzmaurice had struck again.

The scene was one of absolute pandemonium. The area, heavily charged with sulphur dioxide fumes, caused the men to lose control of the refrigerator. Fortunately no one was injured. The resultant pile up of men, equipment and refrigerator at the bottom of the stairs was reminiscent of a Keystone Cop's routine.

The grim faced lieutenant had reserved comment until the unit had returned to quarters. His session in the office with Fitzmaurice had lasted over half an hour. It was only natural that Fitzmaurice would be questioned concerning his ordeal.

On entering the kitchen he'd informed his peers it had been kind of hard to understand the lieutenant. "He was so fucking excited I had a hard time following what he had to say. He kept repeating himself. Something about me having a big fucking mouth. Now, that's something I find hard to believe!"

The lieutenant's comments weren't hard to believe insofar as Fitzie's peers were concerned. "You stupid bastard! You could have got us all killed," was Billy Murray's tart observation. Fitzmaurice was unimpressed. "You're all a bunch of teabags; and that includes the lieutenant." Obviously the lieutenant can count on Fitzmaurice—in the future—insofar as orders at fires are concerned.

As the apparatus pulled up to the vacant lot adjacent to 109th Street and Madison Avenue, Captain Cullen had transmitted a signal 18 indicating the ability of the first arriving Engine and Ladder companies to handle the situation without further help. Stretching a line and extinguishing the small pile of rubbish in the center of the lot had been routine. The package of garbage flung out of the window of a nearby tenement was not. There were a variety of opinions regarding the intent of the perpetrator, and these were undoubtedly influenced by the accuracy of his aim. The huge bag of debris had struck Henderson about the head leaving him dazed, bleary-eyed and outraged. As he stood in the middle of the lot, helmet festooned with dangling toilet paper and coffee grounds, his brief utterance was proof of a Harlem association. "You motherfuckers!"

Being a cautious man, Captain Cullen contacted the dispatcher concerning a medical examination of Henderson. Despite Tom's protestations, the captain was taking no chances. Naturally, Chief McCarthy got into the act. As he arrived at the lot via chief's car, with sirens screaming, bells ringing and brakes screaching, he had immediately taken command of the situation. All evidence would have to be gathered, inventoried and preserved. And so it was.

Tom was examined at the Flower Fifth Avenue Hospital

and placed on medical leave as a precautionary measure. His howls of protest were disregarded. "What the fuck is wrong with everybody? I'm all right. I don't want a medical leave!" The uninitiated will, of course, be impressed by the spartan qualities demonstrated by Henderson. Those in the know will have other thoughts on the matter. The average firefighter moonlights. Economic circumstance makes moonlighting imperative. The department frowns on personnel performing outside work while on medical leave. It's as simple as that.

The inventory of debris associated with the assault on Henderson tabulated and forwarded in quadruplicate consisted of the following:

4 Quart-sized Schaeffer beer bottles, empty
1 Pampers, wet
1 Pampers, brown stained
4 Sanitary napkins, bloodstained
2 Banana peels
7 Cans, empty; labels indicating variety of foods
1 Watermelon rind
1 Pizza box, empty
4 Mango rinds
1 Large brown paper box, obviously enclosing the above listed items.
* The above contents also included a variety of chicken bones, coffee grounds, used toilet paper and one used latex contraceptive device.

This inventory naturally generated discussion concerning the ethnic background of its original owners. The watermelon rind indicated black persons to some. Willie Burrell regarded such assumptions as ridiculous. "What's the matter with you people? Everybody eats watermelon." Fitzmaurice's contention that the pizza box indicated possible Italian complicity was hooted down by Silensa. John's contention that there wasn't an Italian west of Paladin Avenue had validity of a sort. To most, the mango rinds indicated an hispanic culprit. Even Lieutenant DeJesus, assigned to one of the other platoons, was impressed by the mango skins. The rationale was simple. The average anglo wouldn't recognize a mango if they fell over one.

The pile of garbage—now known as "McCarthy's bag of Shit"—remained in a metal can in the yard to the rear of the firehouse. It remained for some four weeks. During its tenure it germinated a huge supply of maggots and an amazingly vile odor. It remained there until the arrival of a Third Grade Detective from the 25th Precinct. His inquiry concerning "that shithead McCarthy" and his statement that he wouldn't touch the evidence with a ten foot pole resulted in a liberal application of Clorox and an eventual disposal of the parcel.

It was Henderson who gained prestige of a sort from the whole matter. His contention that the Medical Office was populated by a gang of assholes met with general approval. His demands for full duty were ignored. "The bastards. They'd send a guy back to work with an arm hanging off! They've cost me two weeks of outside pay out of spite!" Despite Henderson's pique, there were compensations. The formerly unknown and unnamed lot is now known as "Henderson's Lot." Tom likes that. It makes him feel good. A guy has to be valued by his peers in order to have a lot named after him. His instincts are correct. In the entire Harlem area there isn't a place designated McCarthy's lot—or McCarthy's anything else, for that matter. As far as Henderson's concerned, that's justice in the full meaning of the word. It even makes the loss of two weeks moonlighting income all worthwhile.

Visitors From Outer Space

The problems associated with Fireman Henderson and Henderson's Lot have little meaning to persons not actively associated with the fire department. Actually, most people aren't aware of their local firehouses until need arises. Most persons, but not all. There are those few individuals, some rather famous, who regard firehouses and the personnel assigned as unique and worthy of attention. The firefighter—perverse creature that he is—prefers anonymity.

There's a self-imposed segregation adopted by professional firefighters and most civilians find this difficult to understand. The absolute insistence on the part of these men in spending as much off-duty time as possible in each other's company is puzzling to the uninitiated. Psychiatric evaluation will undoubtedly reveal a compulsion requiring those sharing similar hazards to relax together. Whatever the reason, the man who fights fire spends an inordinate amount of time in the company of his peers. Additionally, given the choice, the firefighter would just as soon see the firehouse utilized by those he *expects* to see there. Basically, they have no objections to buffs, firehouse pets and those persons normally expected around the firehouse as a matter of routine. It's the visitor from "Outer Space" that bugs the average member. He resents the presence of characters who have to be treated with kid gloves, those possessing political clout, or sufficient importance requiring that they be handled delicately.

No firehouse is subjected to more visits from Outer Space than the Fire Factory. Politicians desirous of getting their name in print hit there on a regular basis. Journalists short of an idea for a feature story make visits. Foreign visitors feeling a compulsion to compare their own fire departments to an American product, social dilettantes seeking a few cheap thrills, or the writer in search of a plot for a new story, sooner or later beat a path to Harlem's busiest unit.

Fire Factory members are not the only ones anxious to avoid visits to this Harlem firehouse. The brass would much prefer showing off midtown companies, and their rationale is understandable. The midtown area is safer and members assigned to these companies are considered more civilized. Visits to the Fire Factory will be sanctioned only on insistence and only on prior warning to the officer personnel assigned to Engine 58 and Ladder 26. "We got important people visiting your quarters. Keep them fuckin' animals on a tight leash or I'll have your head!"

Naturally, preparations for visits by the prestigious are preceeded by a veritable plethora of committee work. The place is scoured as if for annual inspection and this seldom sits well with the firefighter who is required to extend an extra effort in welcoming persons he'd just as soon not see in the first place. "Why the fuck don't they take in a Broadway show or visit a night club. What are we running here—a goddamned museum?"

Despite protests the place *will* be scoured and despite warnings from the upper echelon, the prestigious *will* often be scandalized or outraged. The reasoning of the Fire Factory member is easy to understand. "I'm here already. Where the hell else are they going to send me?"

It had been an incredibly busy month and the horrendous amount of fire duty indulged in by Harlem units had hit the papers. Not having had his name in print for some time, and badly in need of a plot for a new novel, Oliver Trimble had decided to visit the scene of action. His desire to breathe in the atmosphere necessary to create a plot is understandable. Trimble's an outstanding novelist with an amazing track record of best sellers to his credit. He's also one of America's most publicized homosexuals.

Possessed of a fantastic amount of political and cultural

clout, Trimble would not be put off by the upper echelon's efforts. "No! No! No! I simply will not visit Engine 65 or Ladder 4 or any other trendy midtown fire company. I absolutely insist on seeing these Fire Factory creatures first hand!"

Naturally the phone was busy. Admonitions concerning behavior were passed on to the officer personnel and relayed to their subordinates. Since the firefighter is undoubtedly one of nature's most vigorous heterosexuals, reactions were violent, and none more violent than Gillian's. "Am I to understand that miserable little monstrosity is going to spend the night in these quarters and actually ride the apparatus of Ladder 26?" When assured this information was accurate, Gillian laid down the law. "If Doctor Strangelove makes one move in my direction, I'll hospitalize him!" The reactions of the balance of the platoon were similar. Oscar's rationale that he'd never previously slept in the same room with a "faggot" was buttressed by Silensa's absolute refusal to cook for any "queers!"

It was Captain Cullen who squared things away. Since Trimble's visit was a fait accompli, he decided to make the best of a bad situation and act as graciously towards Trimble as he would to any other visitor. The added admonition concerning his own reactions towards anyone deliberately creating provocations was forceful enough to be effective. John Silensa got the message. He agreed to carry out his normal duties as chef. Additionally, Oscar Ratner resolved to abstain from uttering "faggot" during the period the writer was in quarters.

Things were rather strained for the first hour or so after Trimble's arrival. His insistence on floating around the kitchen, limp wristedly shaking hands with each man, was embarrassing to all but particularly so to Gillian. Looking up at Jim, the writer had observed, "My, you're a big one!" It had taken all of Gillian's self-control to contain himself.

The first run had been a travesty. Trimble had to be physically lifted on to the apparatus. During the run he'd clung to Henderson like a leech. This had caused comment from Tom: "If that fucking run lasted any longer, we'd be engaged!"

As he walked around the scene of the fire in the small bodega on Madison Avenue and East 111th Street, clothed in borrowed fire gear, Trimble looked like a fat leprechaun. The members of the other Harlem units on the scene, aware of Trimble's presence, took every opportunity to harrass the members of the Fire Factory. While the presence of Chief McCarthy did stop them from engaging in overt comment, it did not stop them from actual harrassment. On return to quarters, Captain Cullen was horrified to see chalk marks directly under the tiller seat of Ladder 26. In large letters the message informed all that "TRIMBLE SUCKS." The captain dove ahead of the writer and barely managed to erase the information.

Much to Silensa's annoyance, Oliver insisted in helping with the preparations associated with the meal. Usually John is singing the blues because he can't drum up help. On this occasion he was with a person who knows as much about cooking as he did and he was decidedly uncomfortable. He was heard to say, "I keep thinking the little fuck is gonna turn around and kiss me!"

The meal had been eaten in silence with none of the usual harrassment directed in Silensa's direction. It was Alcock who was the object of Anderson's wrath at the conclusion of the meal. As he dried the dishes, Harry had deliberately dropped and smashed the plate Trimble had used. The lieutenant got the drift immediately. Standing behind Alcock, Anderson whispered, "You smash that little faggot's cup and I'll break your fucking head!"

After the meal, Oliver turned on his tape recorder and proceeded with an attempt to interview members of the platoon. Obviously, he was making an attempt to establish characterizations for use in his novel. Cullen and Anderson left the scene retreating to their respective offices. Their departure was due to a feeling of embarrassment on their parts. It was also a mistake.

The men had a feeling of discomfort in the presence of this character from Outer Space and were not acting normally. Being an extremely intelligent person, Trimble recognized the situation for what it was and took corrective measures.

He left quarters, proceeded to his parked Mercedes and returned with a basket of contraband goodies. The bottles of Chivas Regal, Jack Daniels, Smirnoff and a variety of other alcoholic beverages were placed on the kitchen table. When informed such items were barred from New York City firehouses, he produced a statement from the Fire Commissioner authorizing him to use any effective means of procuring information aimed at the publication of a story associated with the New York City Fire Department. His reasoning was simple: "You dear boys are not opening up—some relaxation is obviously called for!"

The relaxation proceeded for an hour and a half before the sounds of revelry reached the office level. As they were apprised of the situation, Captain Cullen and Lieutenant Anderson decided to hell with consequences. Their rationale was simple enough. If those assholes from downtown want to create situations of this sort, so be it. They joined the party. At 1:15 a.m. Captain Cullen had decided it was time to hit the sack. Prior to heading for the office he procured a piece of chalk and inscribed a message on the apparatus of Ladder 26 directly under the tiller seat.

At 4:10 a.m. both units—including the now resident leprechaun—had responded first, due to what turned out to be a third alarm in a tenement on 116th Street just off Fifth Avenue. The members had performed professionally and Oliver Trimble had secured a host of pertinent information.

Chief McCarthy, proceeding to the chiefs' car prior to returning to quarters, had once more been properly outraged. Chalked on the apparatus of Ladder 26—directly under the tiller seat—was a message, terse and to the point—McCARTHY SUCKS!" An assessment wholeheartedly endorsed by Trimble. "He is a nasty one, isn't he? I'll make him the villain in my book!"

It was a Saturday night and the character with the heavy germanic accent—the one in the company of the department press representative—had arrived in quarters some three hours ago. Joined by Battalion Chief McCarthy and Deputy Chief of Department Wentworth, he'd proceeded to inspect quarters. He was regally presumptuous and managed to find fault with every facet of operation. He'd volunteered suggestions concerning the storage of equipment, usage of masks, maintenance of apparatus and operations at fires. What made the entire episode galling to the Harlem firefighters was Chief McCarthy's insistence on taking notes concerning the guy's every utterance.

The man was invited as a guest for the evening meal and hadn't made any brownie points with Silensa. His insistence on describing Italian cooking, and anything else associated with Italy, as decadent was annoying to John. It was of little significance to John that the visitor was a ranking officer in one of the larger West German fire departments. It was significant that the man had the manners of a boorish lout.

The fire in the basement of the old-law tenement on East 119th Street just off Park Avenue had been the clincher. Captain Cullen and Lieutenant Anderson had been totally satisfied with the performance of their personnel. No one, in their opinion, can handle an old-law tenement fire better than Harlem firefighters. The visitor from Germany begged to differ. He had a host of criticisms ranging from placement of ladders and direction of streams to crowd control. Chief Wentworth was a diplomat and was noncommittal. Chief McCarthy was a brown-nose by nature and agreed with the visitor's every utterance.

Prior to leaving, the German officer had finally given the Fire Factory members the opening they'd been looking for. He asked if any of them had ever been to Germany. He made it sound like Germany was a first cousin to Paradise. Two of the members had made such a visit and were happy to make that fact known.

Lieutenant Anderson had made the tour. "I visited your country as a guest of Uncle Sam. During World War Two I was a member of the 82nd Airborne Infantry!"

Captain Cullen was the other visitor. "During the Big War, I was assigned to a Bomber Group that must have dropped several thousand tons of bombs on your town. It's probably what gave you all that expertise at firefighting. After all—practice does make perfect!"

Chief McCarthy's subsequent tirade had little meaning to either officer. As far as they were concerned the visiting kraut was out of order. The fact that he'd criticized department operations was a minor point hardly worthy of note. He could be excused since he didn't know any better. His boorish treatment of Silensa was something else. No one—as far as Cullen and Anderson are concerned—criticizes John's cooking unless they're a member of the Fire Factory. Sticking the harpoon into Silensa comes with the territory. It's something available only to those on the Fire Factory roster, to those who've earned their spurs. This visitor from Outer Space hardly falls into that category. He simply had to be shafted. And so he was.

George Foster Preston has a very high opinion of himself—and with some justification. For years his expertise as an investigative TV reporter has enabled him to interview the elite. Raking the likes of ex-president Nixon over the coals as millions watched had gained him an enviable reputation. Despite his penchant for harpooning the prestigious, celebrities fight for the privilege of being embarrassed nationally on prime-time by Preston.

Being a busy man, and thoroughly convinced that all work and no play makes George a dull boy, Preston seeks a variety of entertainments. Never one to shun the **limelight**, the man's every move, even when seeking diversion, is aimed at catching the attention of the ever observant Broadway columnist. It's felt by many that Preston's tendency to dally with black girls is aimed at creating comment where it counts.

Naturally the girls he squires are beautiful and talented and none more beautiful and talented than his present flight of fancy, Delia Dunsmore. Singing for her supper in a number of small clubs around the New York Metropolitan area had been merely a means to an end for this girl. She has talent, charm, poise, and sufficient street smarts to realize that hanging around with this honky just might lead to better things.

Delia's a Harlem product and she's come up the hard way. It's certain that if she'd been born male, she'd have used muscle to rise above her environment. Since she's all girl, the curves, the charm, the smile, and the very essence of her femininity are used to claw her way past the competition. Delia's fairly well established now; important people recognize her as a genuine talent. She no longer *has* to stay with Preston, and she's quite capable of making it on her own. The guy is there. He is a man, and he's good for a few laughs. He's a thing of the moment. Who knows what tomorrow may bring.

Prominent among Preston's many talents is his love for the martial arts. He works out regularly and is quite good. While not as good as he thinks he is, the man is far from mediocre. Included in his motif for living is a certain nastiness demonstrated in his TV delivery and in his use of karate at the drop of a hat. Going for the jugular is second nature to Preston. He has no mercy. Give him an opening on his program and you're deep-fried. Cross him personally when he's off the air—particularly when he's been drinking—and you may be hospitalized.

As he rides from Yankee Stadium with Delia and a man from the mayor's office, Preston is annoyed—very annoyed. Reggie'd iced the game by hitting one out of sight. The home run hadn't bothered George. That he could handle. The man's tip of the hat as he rounded third and his obvious wide open invitational grin towards Delia, however, had. To make matters worse, she quite obviously ate it all up.

The mayor's man is handling George's Continental and they're on Fifth Avenue heading south. Immediately in front of the Continental, the apparatus of Ladder 26 heads towards the firehouse. As the huge hook and ladder pulls across the Avenue preparatory to backing into quarters, Delia sees someone she knows. She's out of the automobile in a flash and yelling, "Willie! Willie Burrell! It's me, Delia!"

The spectacle of *his* girl wrapping her arms around the tall, skinny, black firefighter is a bit too much for Preston. He's angry. He reaches into a compartment and brings out a flask. Staring in the direction of the two, Preston takes a long pull, and then another. As far as Preston is concerned, this firefighter had better quit while he's ahead.

Willie had disappeared into the firehouse and Preston figured the incident was at an end. He was wrong. Delia seemed to be waiting at the firehouse door for something. Preston was reaching the end of his fuse.

Angrily the TV personality called from the car. "C'mon, Delia—move it! Let's get the hell out of here!" A year or so ago, Preston's preemptive order would have been instantly obeyed. But she's on her own now; she needs no one. Preston —or anyone else—can watch his mouth as far as this girl is concerned. She glares in Preston's direction and turns her back on the man as Willie comes out of the firehouse door.

It's really all very innocent. Willie has no desire to move in and Delia would never permit it. She makes only those moves that are liable to enhance her career. She's a very practical girl. Willie and Delia continue to stand outside the firehouse cutting up old touches. Preston takes another long pull on the flask.

The two old neighbors stand talking for another minute and Preston leaves the car and walks slowly in their direction. "Nigger, get away from my girl!" The four long pulls on the flask have had their effect and the primitive instincts governing this man are taking control. He continues towards Willie and the girl.

Recognizing the man's mood, Delia barely has time to warn Willie. "Watch him, Willie! He's a karate expert!" The guy's coat is off in a flash. He's prepared for action. Nervously the man from the mayor's office mops his brow with his handkerchief and thinks, "This prick and his karate. Some day I hope he gets the shit beat out of him!"

Willie moves away from the stalking Preston and immediately Preston recognizes Willie's no pushover. The black man's defensive posture demonstrates an advanced knowledge of the martial arts. This only increases Preston's blood lust. He stalks slowly in Willie's direction.

There's a small chink in Preston's armor. All the karate experts he's been up against have appeared in the controlled confines of a dojo. The people he's beaten up in a variety of bars throughout the country were an endless list of toughs possessing no knowledge of the martial arts. Willie Burrell will be something else.

The reporter feints with his left hand and sends a wheel kick aimed at Willie's head. Blocking the blow, Willie slowly retreats towards a parked car. He has a plan in mind and those workouts with Billy Murray are about to pay off. Preston whips a front kick enforced with a punch at Willie's middle and both blows are blocked. Willie allows a blow to glance off his head, fakes distress, and staggers towards the parked car. Preston steps right into the trap and pursues Willie. As they reach the car, Willie leans on the vehicle for support. As Preston moves in, Willie seizes the man's shirt front. Instinctively, Preston pulls back. Willie pulls his opponent back towards him and smashes the outer edge of his right hand over Preston's left clavicle destroying it in the process. It's all over.

The uproar associated with the incident was cataclysmic. The man from the mayor's office—figuring he'd make a hell of a lot more brownie points lying for a celebrity than sticking to the truth—came up with a rather fanciful story.

The media was informed that Preston had decided to visit the Fire Factory in search of material for a program. The firefighter had provoked the situation, according to this toady, and that's the way the press ran the story. It was merely a visit from Outer Space that had backfired.

For a time it looked as if Willie would be out of a job, but then Delia stepped in. Quietly visiting the office of the Fire Commissioner she'd informed him of the true facts. The matter was rather like a nine-day wonder as it disappeared from page one after a time.

Perhaps the most disappointed by the whole incident was Chief McCarthy. He'd filed seventeen charges against Willie ranging in nature from "Leaving Quarters Without Permission" to "Commiting Mayhem on a Civilian." Since all these charges had been prepared in quadruplicate and had taken an inordinate amount of time to prepare, the chief was of the opinion that life simply wasn't fair. He'd worked so hard on these charges and had devoted so much time to their preparation, and now this Burrell character is slipping away scot free. McCarthy has only one consolation. Tomorrow is another day.

For the fourth time in the space of three years, the Fire Commissioner of the City of New York has issued the same directive—"Under no circumstances will visits be sanctioned to the quarters of Engine 58 and Ladder 26!"

Silensa and Ratner are ecstatic. The possibility of respite from visitors from Outer Space enthuses them. Gillian's attitude is more practical. "Don't get your hopes up! It's another fucking nine-day wonder. Like the swallows from Capistrano, them bastards will be back breaking our balls—and you can count on it."

McCarthy is depressed. He considers the possibility of this episode being dropped by the brass as catastrophic. It's so unfair—so very unfair. He consoles himself with thoughts of transfer to more peaceful climes. The transfer application he's forwarded is his twenty-fourth. One for each month he's been assigned to Harlem.

The Rope

The attitude of department members concerning unwanted visitors is often similar to their dislike regarding the introduction of new practices and new materials. Personnel—particularly veteran officer personnel—prefer sticking with the tried and true. Captain Ray Cullen is such a person, and after thirty-three years of fire duty, he's vigorously opposed to learning new tricks.

From a practical standpoint Cullen is an excellent firefighter. His willingness to place his life on the line for others is something he takes for granted. It's part of the job. Such altruism does not necessarily make him a fool.

Never a man for innovation, Cullen tends to stick with devices that have stood the test of time. If a piece of protective equipment has served the department faithfully, it's good enough for Ray Cullen, and thus his conflict with Chief McCarthy.

For years the Manila life rope has served the department and served it well. It's withstood the crucible of time. Ray knows exactly what the rope *can* and what it *can't* do. Since the men assigned to his unit are the ones who will risk their lives, Cullen feels McCarthy's adamant attitude concerning the Manila rope ridiculous.

The captain simply doesn't like the idea of replacing the trusted Manila rope with a substitute he's never seen used at a fire. The fact that laboratory technicians and equipment salesmen wax ecstatic about the new rope's potential cuts no ice with Cullen. Salesmen and technicians never use the rope under emergency conditions.

Cullen is man enough to realize his intense personal dislike for McCarthy may have some bearing on the matter. There is the definite possibility he'd *like* to see McCarthy wrong.

Chief McCarthy has made up his mind insofar as Captain Raymond Cullen of Ladder 26 is concerned. This man will adhere to rules and regulations or pay the penalty. McCarthy is simply appalled that a member of his command would have the audacity to actually debate department policy.

It's part of what the chief considers the Harlem syndrome. The members assigned to this particular area tend to take rules and regulations lightly. Why a preponderance of fire duty should give a man the idea he's exempt from procedures adhered to in other parts of the city escapes McCarthy.

The chief has made up his mind. Tomorrow—not the day after—but tomorrow the Manila rope assigned to Ladder 26 will be removed and forwarded to the department shops. *It will be replaced on a permanent basis by the newly issued nylon rope.*

There will be no further debate on the matter. The fact that Chief McCarthy's superiors feel the need for a change is sufficient. The nylon rope *must* be of higher quality. If it weren't a better piece of equipment, why would the authorities go to the trouble and expense of issuing nylon rope throughout the job?

Tomorrow is D-Day. Tomorrow is the day when Cullen will finally realize just who is running this batallion.

A part of McCarthy hopes Cullen takes further issue with his chief's orders. The opportunity to demonstrate who's boss to the entire batallion might never be presented in more dramatic fashion.

Any chief can rip an ordinary firefighter with three extra watches for straying away from the housewatch area. It would take a real disciplinarian to prefer charges against a captain. McCarthy feels real disciplinarians are the type to reach the very top in this job. Just let Cullen try something tomorrow. Just let him try.

The huddled form at the base of the training tower at the School of Instruction isn't moving. The officer and firemen surrounding the unconscious form are shocked and puzzled. They're shocked because this man is a member of their own unit. A man they like and respect. A family man with responsibilities. They're puzzled because the nylon rope used in the training exercise has snapped plunging one of their members to the base of the tower.

How could this be? Wasn't this the rope everyone in authority praised to the skies? The rope developed and proved infallible by modern technological methods? Some technology!

The ambulance has arrived. The victim has been placed in a Stokes stretcher to lessen the possibility of further bodily damage. The unit members have been cautioned about conversation concerning the rope's failure. Why keep quiet? What's the secret? No explanations. Just keep quiet.

This particular meeting of the brass at headquarters has been called for one purpose. There is only one subject matter on the agenda. The nylon rope will be the subject under discussion—that and nothing else.

Since the stress reports from several reputable laboratories indicate the rope is not all it was cracked up to be, there are those in favor of its instant removal.

Normally the rope would be gone. These are not normal times, however. The injuries suffered by one of the department members in a training exercise are permanent in nature. This man will be retired from the department on a line of duty pension. Throwing out the rope at this point in time could well supply this man's lawyers with ammunition to blast an almost bankrupt city.

Naturally the possibility of further injury has been discussed. Discussed thoroughly. It has been decided that a "keep one's fingers crossed attitude" might be best for the time being. The rope will be replaced at a later date.

The meeting is adjourned. The department's leaders are keeping their fingers crossed.

The all hands fire in the Williamsburg section of Brooklyn had been highlighted by a sensational roof rope rescue by one of the members of Ladder 108.

Using the newly issued nylon rope, one of the members of that crackerjack outfit had been lowered over the roof and successfully removed an hysterically screaming woman from a fourth floor apartment. News media throughout the city had featured this sensational effort. Several members of the brass uncrossed their fingers.

The nylon rope issued to Ladder 26 lies in its compartment. It's tried and tested Manila counterpart sits on the apparatus floor awaiting pickup by a truck from the department shops.

Chief McCarthy is firmly convinced he's demonstrated to Captain Cullen once and for all just who runs this battalion. Captain Cullen is equally convinced Chief McCarthy is a shithead.

The Study Group

Replacement of equipment and changes in procedures are not necessarily the concerns of officer personnel exclusively. Subordinate members, those studying for promotion, are similarly affected. Since new procedures concern these people, study groups have been formed. Considering the almost continuous flow of information emanating from headquarters, such groups are essential.

Actually, study groups are an integral part of most professional fire companies. The tendency of men assigned to individual units to band together in an effort to improve promotional possibilities is recognized and encouraged. Such encouragement is given for a variety of reasons. There are those in authority who are genuinely interested in the effort of younger men to improve their positions. Others, and they are quite a few, operate on the principle that the occupied firefighter is a firefighter temporarily out of trouble.

The Fire Factory has a study group and whether it's encouraged out of a genuine concern for its members is a matter for conjecture. Cullen stands ready to contribute information on request. He's anxious to see his subordinates gain higher rank. Lieutenant Anderson's rationale is somewhat ulterior: "When they're studying I know where those crazy bastards are and what they're doing."

It is a foregone conclusion that any study group will be composed of a diverse group. Here, in these quarters of Engine 58 and Ladder 26, the students range from a high of Gillian and Murray to the decided low of Oscar Ratner.

Gillian has a trememdous intellect and a college-trained mind. Whether this qualifies him to share knowledge with those less intellectually gifted is another matter. His assumption that facts coming easy to him should be at the fingertips of those less gifted can be disturbing. "Oscar, you stupid bastard, if you can't understand square root, how the hell are you going to figure out a hydraulic problem?"

Oscar's rationale that he's been operating complex pumping systems over a period of years without a knowledge of "square root, round root, or any fucking kind of other root" makes sense of a sort. It does not make for a smooth transmission of information within the study group.

Billy Murray is an excellent student. Tried in that intellectual crucible known as the United States Merchant Marine Academy at Kings Point, he'd learned to study the hard way. Entering as a plebe, he'd stuck his nose into a book and kept it there for four years. That was the only way out of that place as far as Billy was concerned. In the process of wrestling with the volume of topics presented, Billy Murray had truly learned how to study. Additionally, being a patient man, he's quite capable of transmitting information to those having more mundane educational backgrounds, an ability sadly lacking in the volatile Jim Gillian.

Since Murray does have patience, it would be only natural that the average member of the study group, desperately trying to master problems readily understood by the college trained, would turn to Murray for assistance. This seldom sits well with Gillian as he is explosive by nature. "What the hell are you asking him for? What is Murray? Some kind of intellectual giant?"

Any group of individuals working toward a common goal will have highs and lows. There will be moments when they're sure they're on the right track. On other occasions they're positive it's all a complete waste of time. Problems will develop. Inability to control discipline within the group will invite disruption. Nothing within this gathering of prospective officers will be more disruptive than the "question fighter." Every group has such an individual. He's the guy impelled to upset routine by haggling over semicolons and commas.

It's possible that the study group within the confines of the Fire Factory is rather unique. They have two question fighters. Which of the two makes a bigger pest of himself is hard to determine. Harry Alcock is one of the question fighters, and his insistence in taking apart the most obscure law, nitpicking over the complexities of words and phrases having little application to any question liable to be asked on any promotion examination, is maddening. Larry Fitzmaurice is the other nuisance and he's felt by many to be an even greater disturbance than Alcock. His tendency to read items into study material not there in the first place comes close to driving Gillian up the wall.

Fitzmaurice's arrival on one particular evening can be taken as an example. He came to clear up a problem that was greatly disturbing to him. He'd been reading a portion of Chapter 19 of the Administrative Code and was stumped by a section dealing with flammable solvents. As usual, he's speeded through the material, covering the entire chapter in a matter of moments. The problem scheduled for discussion that evening concerned the rather complicated fire hazards found in some of the large "H" shaped buildings in the Riverdale section of the Bronx. Larry refused to allow discussion to be started until such time as his problem was thoroughly cleared up.

"I don't give a fuck about "H" shaped buildings. What I want to know is how come raisins are flammable?" There was a silence for a moment as the group tried to digest the import behind Larry's demand. Patiently going through the index associated with Chapter 19, Billy Murray had been unable to find any indication of a heading under raisins. Fitzie was almost scornful. "You and your college education—it's right under flammable solvents!"

It was Gillian who first became aware of Fitzie's problem. "The stupid son of a bitch is confusing raisins with resins. How the hell are we going to conduct a study group of any consequence with morons of this type? I'm out of the group right here and now!" Fitzie's offer to punch out Jim's lights was hardly conducive to an exchange of intellectual information. Nor was Gillian's willingness to accept Fitzmaurice's challenge. The class was disbanded for the day.

There are, of course, other disturbing factors associated with attempts at advancement. The insistence of those in higher ranks to help by supplying information no longer valuable to the modern student can be trying. Lieutenant Anderson hasn't studied for years. While there isn't a better engine company officer in the job, time has passed the man by insofar as some of the complexities of modern test taking are concerned. "Hey, guys, here's some stuff I dug out of a closet at home!" Since he's a hell of a nice guy and also the man in charge, an entire half hour can be wasted while he goes over material no longer relevant. Gillian's observation that someone should tell the man "his information is as useless as tits on a bull" falls into the category of just what mouse shall place the bell on the cat.

Other sources of annoyance to those inclined towards study are found in the childish efforts at disruption offered by those not interested in advancement. Brennan, not eligible for the next lieutenant's test, and Henderson, who simply can't work up sufficient enthusiasm to make the effort, find it necessary to make pests out of themselves. Their insistence on singing loudly and in chorus adjacent to the study group is annoying. The group considers downright insulting that their choral selection is always that old time favorite "Am I Wasting My Time." The results are inevitable; Gillian blows a fuse and makes threats.

"Stop that fucking caterwauling or I'll punch the shit out the pair of you!"

"It's a free fucking country and we got as much right to sing as you jerks have to study!"

Usually matters are straightened out by Captain Cullen and his reminders to the choral society. His suggestion that those with sufficient time on their hands to break chops might possibly be utilized more productively has results. When given a chance of shining poles or refraining from making nuisances of themselves, the pair always get the message.

Silensa can be disturbing. His insistence on approaching the group to request information concerning the following day's menu can be disruptive. Naturally, it's Gillian who hits the ceiling. "Cook any goddamned thing you want! Just get the fuck out of here! We're right in the middle of a complex situation concerning those idiot Queen Anne-type buildings they've got over in Flatbush and we don't need any annoyance from you!"

John is not easily put aside. "You were the guy screaming his lungs out about the cost of today's meal! I want some information from you as to just how I can lower costs! Now, let's get things straightened out! Would you prefer stuffed peppers or should I concentrate on a minestrone soup? It seems to me the further I stay away from meat, the cheaper the meal!"

Gillian's reaction never varies. Rising to his full six-foot-five inches, arms raised imploringly skyward, he shouts, "COOK ANY FUCKING THING YOU WANT!"

Lack of patience is hardly limited to Gillian. Others are quite capable of volatile reaction. Pudgy Dunn—soon to be promoted—has been expelled from the group for disruptive behavior. His opinion that his place on the lieutenants' list and the strong possibility that he'd be eligible for the next captains' exam gave him the authority to supervise the curriculum selected had met with violent reaction.

I'm the guy with proven results and I'm the guy that's going to decide what this group covers!" Fitzmaurice's reply hardly endeared him to Pudgy. "You're the guy that should have been playin' the horses on the day of that last examination. You guessed your way through half of that bullshit test!"

Pudgy's reactions are understandable for a change. He's a good student and his place on the list is far from accidental. He's applied himself and he's about to be promoted on merit. "Fuck you, Fitzmaurice—they don't call you the Fire Hydrant because of your shape. It's because you and the hydrants have no fucking brains! Now, let's get things straight. I'm the guy in charge of this group or I quit." They never gave Pudgy the chance to quit. They threw him out of the group permanently.

For a while Pudgy sulked. The embarrassment of being ejected from anything associated with fire department activity hurt him deeply. He did console himself with the thought that he could take the books down into the basement and pound away without Alcock driving him crazy concerning some obscure provision of the Labor Law. He'd also be free of Oscar's attempts to master fourth grade multiplication problems. Nor would he miss Fitzmaurice's constant misinterpretation of the printed word. For a while he considererd revenge. He considered joining Brennan and Henderson in one of their songfests, but discarded the idea as childish. He thought of the possibility of returning to the Fire Factory and having his revenge by strutting around quarters wearing a white hat while supervising company activity. However, the mere thought of placing himself in a category even remotely resembling Chief McCarthy was enough to drive this thought out of his mind.

Finally, he decided to swallow his pride. He'd ask the guys to take him back into the group on their terms. It wasn't that he needed any of the knowledge possessed by the group; after all, he was on the lieutenants' list. It was simply his desire to be part of anything associated with company activity. Pudgy's a joiner. He has to be part of the group. He's also a damned fine firefighter with a true feeling of affection for anything remotely associated with the Fire Factory.

The guys beat him to the punch. They invited *him* back. Naturally, they had to drive him insane in the process. Keeping as straight a face as possible, Billy Murray informed Pudgy he was being asked back because of his superior knowledge in one aspect of firefighting not possessed by the average Harlem firefighter.

Pudgy has a weak spot. He wasn't appointed in Harlem. For four months he had been a member of an obscure Queens company specializing in grass fires. Those attempting to drive him mad over the matter seldom considered that he'd battled his way out of such an environment as rapidly as possible.

Once Pudgy expressed his desire to be readmitted to the group on any terms, Billy stuck it to him. "We're terribly concerned they may have questions about grass fires on the test and you're the only guy in quarters with extensive experience in the matter!"

Outraged, Pudgy began screaming at the top of his lungs, so loudly that the subject matter was easily discernible outside the quarters. "Grass—what the fuck do I know about grass! I was only in Queens for four months. If you want to know about grass, call up that prick McCarthy. Don't ask me about grass—I don't know a goddamned thing about grass!"

The two teenagers walking past quarters paused briefly to listen to Pudgy's outburst. For a moment, they were puzzled. Finally, one of them came to a conclusion. "They havin' some sort of trouble with their delivery of marijuana from Queens. Seems their main man McCarthy ain't comin' through for them!"

The lighter skinned of the two, shrugging his shoulders, starts south on Fifth Avenue. "That's their problem, man! I got enough trouble gettin' my own shit together! Things is tough all over! It's that Mayor Koch, man! He's closin' everything up tighter than a drum!"

His friend agrees: "You right, brother, that Koch is a rough dude! We gotta get rid of him. When he closes the lid down on the fire department, what the hell chance we got? Yeah, we gotta get rid of him fast."

The Nine Alarmer

Firefighters face a range of problems. Men involved with the mundane matters of a study group today may well be concerned with life and death tomorrow. Since fires—like the very firefighters who fight them—come in all sizes and shapes, it's only natural that circumstances that can amaze even the most blase of Harlem's protective forces should eventually develop. This bitter winter evening is such an occasion.

Regardless of weather, the men assigned to Engine 58 and Ladder 26 seldom concern themselves with apparatus response. If they remain in quarters, it's a plus. If an alarm hit in, it's part of the job. Tonight is no exception. Here, in the kitchen of this Harlem firehouse, they are of one mind. Their combined thought processes are best expressed by Fitzmaurice's: "Keep the fuckin' brass monkeys in tonight."

It's not the recorded Central Park temperature of minus one that bothers these men. That they can handle. The 40-mile-per-hour wind howling down from the north with its windchill factor of minus 30 degrees is something else. Tonight's a night for the wife, the kids and the fireplace. It's a night for television or a good book. Given the opportunity, there isn't a man assigned for duty who wouldn't head for home. No one in his right mind looks forward to getting wet tonight. The prospect is enough to send chills up the spine of every member of these ghetto units.

They've been out three times and each run was an agony. Two of the responses were false alarms. Just searching the area for possible cause reddened the face and teared the eye.

The call for the fire in the small pile of rubbish was cause for alarm. The fire hydrant they'd attempted to use was frozen solid. Just extinguishing this minor fire had been a problem. The streets are packed with ice from last week's nine-inch snowstorm. Stretching two lengths along a flat surface had taken minutes longer than normal. The men were slipping and sliding in all directions and the possibility of serious injury was staring each man in the face. The two lengths of stretched hose had frozen solid in moments, leaving little to the imagination concerning the weather's reaction at a larger fire.

On each occasion the return to quarters had been an adventure. Automobiles were skidding in all directions. Pedestrian traffic inched along with every fifth person slipping on ice-glazed sidewalks. If ever there was a night when each and every man of these units prays for a tour free of major activity, this is that night.

Mindful of the weather, Silensa has determined that minestrone soup will be served. The preparations are lengthy and the possibility of anyone eating prior to nine-thirty leaves most of these firefighters more than a little testy. Even that pair of martial arts stalwarts, Burrell and Murray, have bowed to the elements. They've postponed their karate workout for the first time in the memory of anyone assigned to this platoon. Their logic is simple. Turning out into this frigid atmosphere in sweat-soaked clothing would be inviting pneumonia.

The seven-thirty news had been far from cheerful. Three fires had been featured. Two in the Bronx and one on the Brooklyn waterfront had presented ice encrusted apparatus presided over by firefighters looking like apparitions from outer space. The unspoken "better you than me" had been buttressed by silent prayers and crossed fingers. "Please, God, not tonight!"

Every man wears long winter underwear and heavy socks. Each turnout coat has an extra pair of gloves. Several of the men have provided themselves with earmuffs. They're prepared and they're edgy and ready to vent their anger on anyone. The company chef is a handy object. While certainly he has nothing to do with the weather, the meal is late. Gillian is hungry—very hungry. "When the fuck are we going to eat? I'm starving." The usually mild mannered Silensa is not in a good mood. "You'll eat when I get goddamned good and ready to put the meal on the table!"

Radio traffic is heavy. Apparatus is being routed all over Manhattan. There's an All Hands fire in the Times Square area and another one down near the Bowery. A host of small working fires, interspersed with the usual mindless false alarms, keep the apparatus on the move.

Closer to home, Engine 69 and Ladder 28 have reported "one and one" working with the rest of the units standing fast. A second alarm is reported in the Riverdale section of the Bronx and there's a call for Department Ambulance One. A firefighter operating at the All Hands fire in the Bowery has fallen from a ladder and broken a leg.

It's nine-thirty and the minestrone is ready. The soup plates are filled and the bread sliced about the time box 1664 is transmitted. Since neither unit is scheduled for response on the first alarm, the signal has little significance. The reaction to the special call for the 12th Battalion, dragging Chief McCarthy out into the cold to supervise activities at that spot is best expressed by Lieutenant Anderson. "I hope he freezes his balls off!"

Gillian is on his fourth serving when the All Hands for box 1664 is transmitted. It causes a momentary stir as both units are assigned on the third alarm. Given the probable odds there's still a good chance of lucking out, McCarthy's penchant for covering his hide is well known. That "All Hands" will bring in a ranking officer. McCarthy will be off the hook from making vital decisions.

Ten minutes pass and the guys are feeling lucky. The kitchen's warm, the minestrone tops, stomachs are pleasantly full and all seems well with their part of the world. Like all good feelings, it has to end. The dispatcher's adamant demand for Progress Report Number One alerts these Harlem firefighters to the possibility of response. The shortage of ranking personnel has left box 1664 in McCarthy's hands. As usual, he's delayed his report hoping to dump that responsibility in someone else's lap.

The report is awesome. Two seven-story apartment buildings are involved. The top three floors of each structure are showing flame. The progress report hadn't even been completed. The arriving Deputy Chief of Department had banged out a second alarm on arrival.

Individual reaction to this developing situation varies. Several men rush for the urinal, a reasonable precaution considering the possibilities confronting them. Others hit for their lockers and a variety of heavy clothing. Some struggle into extra pairs of pants, woolen undershirts and sweaters. Their precautions are sensible. The third alarm, dragging them out into the nightmare of sub-freezing temperature, is transmitted at 10:08 p.m.

As Engine 58 inches out of quarters, the blast of arctic air hitting Lieutenant Anderson chills him to the bone. Never has he felt so cold. The apparatus proceeds north on Fifth Avenue at a snail's pace. Vehicular traffic is in trouble. There's a fender bender a block from quarters and two drivers argue vehemently. Another car, obviously abandoned, blocks two lanes. The apparatus turns left on 116th Street and is met by two snowball throwing imbeciles. Fortunately, all of the ice-laden missiles miss the firefighters.

Turning right on Seventh Avenue, Anderson can hear Progress Report Number Two on the department radio. One of the buildings is fully involved and the second isn't in much better shape. The fourth alarm has been transmitted with an admonition to the dispatcher. The terse "doubtful will hold" leaves little to the imagination.

They've been out of quarters ten minutes as they reach 125th Street. Normally they'd be stretching a line by now. With a full mile of response to go, Anderson keeps his feet jammed down on the siren button. There isn't a driver on the street whose car windows aren't shut tight. Under the circumstances it's simply better to slow down. Becoming involved in an accident would make no sense and the apparatus crawls slowly north.

When the huge hook and ladder of Ladder 26 cleared quarters, Captain Cullen made sure the apparatus door was closed. Bringing back a soaking wet crew to an ice cold quarters simply wouldn't make sense.

Ahead the captain can see the slowly moving vehicle assigned to Engine 58. Obviously, Lieutenant Anderson has ordered moderate speed, a sensible precaution Cullen has every intention of following. Maneuvering the apparatus through the variety of stalled traffic takes the combined skills of chauffeur Silensa and the tillerman Gillian. The situation isn't helped by the snowball throwing cretins at 116th Street. For a moment he considers stopping the apparatus for the purpose of busting a few heads, but he decides to forego the pleasure. Turning into Seventh Avenue Gillian has rough time with the tiller. The rear of the apparatus is all over the street. Fortunately, there's no traffic alongside. Engine 58 is half a block ahead. Cullen orders Silensa to maintain just that interval of distance for the balance of the trip.

Hanging on to one of the safety straps at the rear of Engine 58's apparatus, Bernie Schwartz agrees with his wife. At least once a day since his assignment to this Harlem unit, the girl he married for better or worse has informed him, "Bernie, you're out of your mind!" Now, with the wind doing its best to blow him off the back step, he's in complete agreement. Never has the insurance business been more lucrative! Never has there been less reason for taking the physical pounding he's been subjected to since his arrival at Engine 58. As the apparatus passes 135th Street, Bernie huddles close to the massive Fitzmaurice—anything for a little warmth. His wife is absolutely right. Bernie Schwartz is out of his mind.

Holding on to the running board of Ladder 26, Pudgy Dunn is outraged. It's not the weather that bothers him. There's nothing he can do about the weather. He'd been walloped by a snowball, but that isn't the cause of his discontent. He considers the source.

It's the guys he works with that bother him. Here he is a man on the lieutenants' list and they treat him like a moron. As the apparatus grinds slowly along, Pudgy broods over that phone call. Who can it be? If he finds out, he'll call the guy out. He'll punch out the guy's lights.

When the phone rang, Pudgy had been called to the housewatch desk and he stepped right into the wise guy's trap. "Are you Dunn?" the caller asked. When Pudgy had replied in the affirmative, the son-of-a-bitch had lowered the boom. "In that case, wipe your ass and pull the chain!"

Standing at the housewatch desk, phone in hand, feeling like a horse's ass, Pudgy had never been angrier. Now with the wind howling down Seventh Avenue, he has just one request. "Please, God, let me know who that bastard is and help me get assigned as a lieutenant in his company!"

Lieutenant Anderson can spot the fire now. It's a roaring inferno. Two huge apartment complexes are fully involved. The lieutenant recognizes the buildings. Constructed in the early part of the century for luxury living, they're occupied by fairly affluent blacks. Occupying the entire block between 143rd and 144th Streets, they're elevator apartments rented by cops, firemen, school teachers and post office employees on their way out of the ghetto. For the time being they'll also be out of living quarters.

Pulling into the fire block, Captain Cullen and Lieutenant Anderson report in to Chief McCarthy. He's his usual charming self. "Sure took you people long enough to get here!" Ladder 26 is ordered to the roof of one of the involved buildings to assist in the necessary ventilation. It's a reasonable enough order under the circumstances. McCarthy's orders to Lieutenant Anderson are something else. Engine 58 will stretch a line up the aerial of Ladder 40 and direct a stream into the top floor of one of the heavily involved buildings. Lieutenant Anderson regards the order as asinine. The ladder will be coated with ice and the buildings sufficiently involved to be written off. Like most department personnel, Anderson regards the life of a firefighter as expendable only when life is at stake and answers, "Chief, that's like pissing off pier six. What the hell good are we going to do up there?" McCarthy is adamant. Engine 58 will operate from just that position.

Engine 80 is connected to a hydrant across the street from

the fire building. Since the Motor Pump Operator of that outfit can supply another line, the members of Engine 58 will stretch in from that location. Anderson can see three deckpipes dumping heavy volume streams into the buildings. The effects are negative. The spray from the deckpipes has iced up the metal rungs of the ladder. Anderson can barely make the climb. He wonders how his crew will be able to stretch a line under these circumstances. He wonders how a man could reach the rank of Battalion Chief and still be stupid enough to risk the lives of personnel needlessly. Reaching the top floor area, Anderson can see nothing but a sea of flame. He snaps the safety clasp of his life belt onto the rung and waits for his crew to complete their perilous stretch.

Billy Murray has hooked his life belt to the ice encrusted ladder. Laboriously, he hauls on the hose line. As strong as he is, this is an exhausting task. Looking up, he can see Fitzmaurice struggling around the lieutenant in order to get into position. When the line is finally in place, Murray secures his section to the aerial via hose strap.

Since he has to climb further up the ladder, Murray attempts to unhook his life belt but the damned thing is frozen solid. As Murray struggles with both hands to free himself, the hook suddenly flies free. Slipping on the ice-encrusted rung Billy comes close to losing his balance. For a terrifying moment he hangs half on and half off the ladder. He's panic stricken. The wild, howling wind seems to seize him. Never has he been so frightened. Looking around he sees flame gushing from every window. Every fiber of his being demands he climb down from that ladder. Looking up he can see Schwartz, Alcock and Brennan slowly crawling upward. Spray from one of the deckpipes saturates him, freezing instantly as Bill clings to the ladder. Each moment is a torment. Bill thinks first of his wife and kids and then of his father. "This is the way the old man made his living. I know what he'd want me to do!" He starts up the ladder.

For Jack McBride this is his first really big fire. He's been to any number of All Hands jobs and even a few second alarms. This is a big one. Now, detailed to Ladder 26 for the tour, he's been assigned to the portable saw and in company with the rest of the platoon he follows Captain Cullen. He's puzzled. He can't understand why they're proceeding down a side street. Henderson's explanation clears up his problem. They'll proceed to an uninvolved building, climb up to its top floor and gain access to the roof of one of the burning buildings in an attempt to ventilate.

When he reaches the roof, McBride is close to panic. Never has he been in such a situation. At this height the wind howls eerily. Spray from the deckpipes below ices up the turnout coats of every man operating at this location. It's almost a pleasure to start working—anything to warm one's body. Assigned a portion of the roof, McBride starts the saw. His gigantic frame has enough energy to do an excellent job and he opens up a large portion of the roof, releasing volumes of heat, smoke and flame.

Perhaps a man of more experience would have become aware of the sponginess of the roof sooner. Captain Cullen had issued a definite order to retreat. The howling wind and McBride's intense attack of the roof surface trap him. He hasn't heard the order. The roof is starting to go. He drops the saw and runs. It's like running on a mattress; he makes hardly any headway. Flames are pushing through the roof surface.

Where is everyone? Where have they all gone? He rests for a moment. He's totally disoriented. The other roof—where is it? In which direction should he turn? One of his boot-clad legs plunges through the weakened roof. He pulls frantically, finally releasing his leg. He's in panic. "Help me! Help me! Help me!"

Engine 58 has its line in position. Lieutenant Anderson's first thoughts were concerned with operating the nozzle himself. The idea of one of the men passing him on this ice-encrusted ladder seems too dangerous. Fitzmaurice had simply climbed around and over him assuming his position as nozzleman.

Knowing damned well that Fitzmaurice had deliberately chosen to ignore a direct order, the lieutenant still feels a tremendous sense of pride in his men. Tradition is everything for an Engine Company. Non-officer personnel will operate the nozzle. Never—Never will they surrender that nozzle.

The stream seems pitifully inadequate as it disappears without effect into the fiery interior. Water from the deck and ladder pipes pours onto the crew of Engine 58 and freezes instantly. Silently, Anderson, soaked to the bone, curses Chief McCarthy. Debris from the cockloft tumbles down bouncing off the ladder and off the huddled members.

Each man is secured to the ladder via his own life belt. Each man has used a hose strap to secure a portion of the hose line to the ladder. It occurs to Anderson that these men could actually be used to advantage in other portions of this huge fire. Certainly they're accomplishing nothing of any value in this position.

Time passes agonizingly slowly. The wind howls and Anderson suffers intensely. As the lieutenant peers into the upper floor, he becomes aware of an alarmingly perilous situation. He sees that several huge supporting beams, normally anchored into front and back walls, are hanging loose. There is only one cause for this situation—the front wall has pulled away from the beams and is ready to go.

There's no way Anderson is going to waste time seeking advice or permission in this potentially deadly situation. His duty is to the men he commands. Ordering the line shut down, he and the men proceed to the street. His welcome is far from cordial.

Chief McCarthy, outraged as usual, was in the process of screaming vitriolic comments about charges, obeying orders and resuming former positions when the wall let loose with a roar. The members of Engine 58 began diving in all directions. The apparatus of Ladder 40 was smashed flat as a pancake. Billy Murray was the only casualty. Diving from the apparatus platform of Ladder 40, he sprained his back.

When the crew of Engine 58 had reported into Chief McCarthy, Oscar Ratner had driven the apparatus in search of a hydrant. Amazingly, he'd spotted the top of a hydrant buried in snow. The hydrant was directly across from one of the involved buildings and had been missed by earlier arriving units. Oscar's spotting the nearly buried hydrant was pure luck. He grabbed a shovel, cleared the hydrant, and made his connection as rapidly as possible. He'd managed to supply two fourth alarm companies with lines and finally set up and operated the deck pipe of Engine 58.

As he aimed his stream in the direction of a heavily involved third floor window, Oscar was amazed to see the men from his unit stretch a line up a heavily iced ladder. That they involved themselves in this hazardous maneuver amazed Ratner.

When the wall came down, Oscar was positive his friends were still on the ladder. He was shocked. To be the only surviving member of a platoon is too much. "Fuck this job" is Oscar's reaction. Who needs a job like this? Let someone else take the grief. He swore to retire tomorrow at 9:00 a.m.

It was Willie Burrell who first realized McBride's dilemma. Staying as close to the parapet as possible, he'd held a six foot hook in the big man's direction. Hanging on to the hook, McBride managed to reach the parapet wall. Hauling themselves along the wall the pair had managed to reach the safety of the adjoining roof. There was no time for the men assigned to Ladder 26 to concern themselves with McBride's narrow escape. The unit was required elsewhere. They'd been ordered to proceed to the street level and assist in the stretching of a hand line.

As they hurried down the stairs, they were greeted with a wild rumor. There's been a collapse involving the members of Engine 58. Suddenly they felt colder, much colder.

Assistant Chief of Department George Robinson is the highest ranking black in the job. A member for over thirty years, he'll hang around until they throw him out. He loves this job and its personnel. Prior to his appointment, he'd delivered groceries—when he could get a job. He owns his own home now. It's far from this Harlem ghetto. He'll never forget Harlem and he has mixed emotions about the place, lots of fond memories and lots of hard times.

Robby's been on the run all night. Racing from one fire to another, he's never been prouder of his men. He feels for the guys. This is a rough night and he knows they're suffering.

Getting out of the chief's car, Robinson regards the awesome spectacle. In his thirty-odd years he's been to few fires to match its intensity. Two buildings fully involved attacked by a variety of deckpipes, ladder pipes, cherry pickers and play pipes. He knows the buildings. He knows them well. He's visited friends here many times. Partying here had always been a pleasure. These had been good buildings with good people as tenants.

He looks around at the lines being stretched. The guys are having a rough time with the ice, the snow, the bitter cold wind. These are his men and they're tops.

The fifth alarm is in and these two buildings are showing flame from every window on every floor. Robby, considering the possibility of calling for further help, rivets his attention on a raised, ice-encrusted ladder. To his utter consternation, he can see a crew backing down that aerial. "What the hell are they doing in a spot like that?"

He starts to walk hurriedly. Those men are in danger. He can see a white helmeted figure berating a company officer as the last of the men reach the turntable of the apparatus.

As the wall comes down, Chief Robinson has made up his mind. Whoever placed those men in that perilous position will have the hide verbally ripped off his back piece by piece.

The TV cameraman pointing his portable camera towards the ice-encrusted fire chief being interviewed by Channel Seven's roving reporter wishes they'd wrap up this job and get the hell back down town.

This is the fourth one of these spectacles he's been to tonight, and if he never sees an ice-encrusted firefighter again it will be too soon.

Yes, they are heroic. *Yes*, they all do a fabulous job. *Yes*, they'd just escaped getting killed by the goddamned falling wall. *Yes*, there had been nine fucking alarms transmitted, and *Yes*, my balls are frozen stiff, so how about getting the fuck out of here.

It's 8:00 a.m. on this bitter cold morning. Nine alarms had been transmitted and now this fire is finally under control. Many of the units have returned to quarters. Both buildings are gigantic icicles. The apparatus is ice-encrusted and the firefighters barely able to move. Members of the media have left. Spectacular footage has appeared on all local TV stations. The injured have been removed to a number of hospitals. Thankfully, nothing more serious than lumps, bumps and a variety of bruises has been sustained. Perhaps the most serious damage has been inflicted on Chief McCarthy's ego. To quote Lieutenant Anderson: "Robby chewed his ass out!"

Several decisions and one conclusion have been reached by a few of the members of Engine 58 and Ladder 26, undoubtedly inspired by this monumental fire and the inclement weather. Oscar Ratner will definitely retire. He sees the handwriting on the wall. Bernie Schwartz will *not* retire. He feels useful.

Pudgy Dunn's the one with the reached conclusion. For an inordinate amount of time he's been trying to remember just who Chief McCarthy resembles: "That jerk reminds me of that creep Frank Fucking Burns from that TV show *MASH*. He's every bit as stupid and even more useless!" An assessment heartily endorsed by every firefighter assigned to the Harlem area.

Fun and Games

It's not all work for the members of the Fire Factory. Recreational activities are definitely part of the norm. Considering their personalities, it's highly unlikely they'd submit to the discipline required to extinguish, or at least assist in the extinguishment of a nine-alarm fire, without seeking some form of relaxation.

Since firefighters are a far from normal group, recreational pursuits will be far from mundane. Some might say that in their retreat from the norm, firefighters' recreational activities approach the bizarre.

To those close to the firefighter, the similarity between combat troops and fire department personnel is apparent. The members of these disparate groups are well aware that they may be expendable. Thus, both the serviceman on leave and the firefighter on an off-tour may engage in recreational activities normally frowned upon. Tearing up a bar in the rear echelon would hardly be fun unless accompanied by members of one's own platoon. Similarly, the firefighter prefers to relax in the presence of his peers. That such relaxation may at times become boisterous is merely coincidental.

There is one small difference concerning these escapes from reality. The combat serviceman rarely returns to the same spot. Not so for the firefighter. He often returns to the scene of the crime. Whether these encores are a welcome addition to the selected neighborhood is a matter for conjecture.

Zephyr Point is an outstanding example of an area receiving constant visitation by fun loving firefighters. Located near the tip of the Rockaway peninsula, it's a colony of summer bungalows. These dwellings are occupied by white middle class Americans with preconceived notions concerning just what makes the good old U.S. of A. tick. To quote Gillian, "Those bastards make Archie Bunker seem like a screeching liberal!"

Entrance to this enclave is afforded only to those living there and their guests. No one passes these well-guarded portals without being thoroughly scrutinized. The entire area is patrolled by a private police force with very definite notions concerning who—and who will not—be admitted!

Pudgy Dunn owns one of these bungalows. It's been in the Dunn family for years. Actually, the bungalow's location is the primary cause for many of Pudgy's late firehouse arrivals. Despite his vigorous denunciation of the FDR Highway, it's the bungalow and its Zephyr Point environs that cause most of his tardiness. Pudgy loves the surf, the sand, the brew and all the other goodies associated with Zephyr Point. He loves them so much he delays his departure to the point of insanity. Thus his frequent late arrivals.

Being generous by nature, Pudgy allows the members of Engine 58 and Ladder 26 to use the Dunn bungalow for "Fun and Games." Such usage always occurs in September after the Dunn children have returned to school. Preparations concerning food are, of course, Silensa's baby. No one in their right mind would attempt to usurp his prerogatives. The variety of hot dogs, hamburgers, beans, cold beets, potato salad, cole slaw, potato chips, pretzels and numerous other foods are assembled and prepared under his supervision. Interspersed with a melange of Neopolitan maledictions concerning the impossibility of preparing a meal "with all this fucking sand flying around" comes his inevitable threat to quit cooking for these animals. Somehow John has attended eight consecutive Zephyr Point beach parties without coming close to engaging in any activity other than the preparation of food.

Getting most of the members past the gate is hardly a problem. Pudgy simply leaves the names of his guests and they're admitted without question—with one exception. Willie Burrell is the man standing out like a sore thumb. Past attempts to convince gate-tending personages concerning Willie's being Italian, an American Indian, an Indian-type Indian from India, a member of the ambassadorial staff from Bangladesh, and several other imaginative ploys have proven fruitless. Not that Willie has ever missed the festivities. He'd simply been secreted under the food, beer and supplies and brought to where he has every right to be in the first place.

Now no one in his right mind connected with the administrative staff of Zephyr Point will admit to prejudice. They're emphatic on that point. There's no prejudice. However, it's private property and unless a person's name is on the guest list they won't be admitted. Somehow the names of black guests appearing at Zephyr never seem to be on the roster furnished the gatekeeper. It's all very mysterious.

Being competitive by nature, it's fitting that these firefighters would indulge in a softball game. Softball and beach parties seem to go together. There's a friendly rivalry of sorts between these units and it's only natural that the Engine Company play the Ladder Company. Since firefighters are unusual, it follows that the rules of the game will vary from the norm. A barrel of beer adjoins third base and any man heading for home is required to down a beer before attempting to score. While this tends to keep the contest close, the resulting traffic jams on the bases lead to violent arguments, triple plays, any number of men standing on the same base and quantities of spilled beer.

On a beautiful September morning the arriving Harlem picnickers found a fly in the ointment. The ball field was occupied by another fire department group. Some consideration had been given to the prospect of possibly playing this outfit for a keg of beer. Attempts at camaraderie were defeated by Pudgy's rather belligerent attitude concerning firefighters assigned to non-hazardous areas. "They're from Whitestone fucking Queens! Let's set up our game down on the beach!"

During summer months the beach is jammed. Once the summer crowd leaves, it's a beautiful expanse of sand pounded by a ceaseless surf. There's a surfcaster up the beach on this day. Overhead there's a flock of squalling gulls protesting

Joshua,

This is a U.S. Air Force flight suit, worn by a jet pilot.

Merry Christmas

Love, Dave, Maureen

CHRISTMAS 1962

vigorously. Far out at sea a tanker plows steadily ahead and two small craft troll for blues. It's a truly beautiful day.

The game had progressed to the fourth inning with Engine 58 in the lead by three runs. Gillian's assertion that Pudgy's insistence on pitching because he owns the bungalow can only lead to disaster is vigorously disputed. "For a guy that's made three fucking errors, you've got a lot to say."

A large quantity of beer had been consumed and the men were having a good time. The usual confusion on the basepaths, largely created by the keg adjoining third base, merely added to the fun. Usually the game would have been finished. A few of the men would have had a swim and the exodus to the bungalow barbeque would have taken place. This was not an ordinary day.

Alcock was the first to spot the uniformed figure advancing in their direction. While the private cop's uniform was certainly not unusual, his size was. If he towered over five-foot-two, it would be giving him the benefit of the doubt. "Looks like a Barnum and Bailey fucking clown," was the way Pudgy expressed himself.

Certainly the man was no diplomat. Neither could he be charged with common sense. Drawing himself up to his full height and pointing at Willie Burrell, he'd made an announcement that seemingly had gone out of style with the arrival of the Civil Rights Amendment. "You guys know there's no niggers allowed here! Get him out of here right now!"

Willie wasn't the one removed. Approaching this miniature cop, Gillian, Murray, Brennan and Fitzmaurice had picked him up and sprinted toward the surf. After flinging the cop out as far as possible, they patiently waited while he plowed his way ashore. They flung him out again, only desisting when their companions insisted on their turn. The event shortly turned into an Engine vs. Ladder contest for distance, form and style. The guy damned near drowned.

Naturally, there were repercussions. Two weeks later Pudgy sadly appeared at the firehouse with a written notice. "I've been asked to move from Zephyr Fucking Point!"

It would be stretching the imagination to assume that fun

and games for these Harlem firefighters are limited to Zephyr Point. There are other forms of activity. There's Super Bowl Sunday. It's a well-known fact that the United States of America closes down on this particular day. Certainly there are people who regard the proceedings associated with these few hours of mayhem as close to a religious experience. Apart from the purely athletic side of this pageant, a tradition has developed. Super Bowl parties are held from one end of the nation to the other. Since the members of Engine 58 and Ladder 26 are definitely part of the American scene, they honor the tradition. The day is spent at Billy Murray's.

Football is a male experience for the most part and Maureen Murray is decidedly female. This particular annual activity actually removes three months yearly from her life span. The two months preceding the game are spent in total apprehension as to just what will happen to her home *this* year. The extra month is devoted to restoring a semblance of order to a house rendered a shambles by some thirty stampeding firefighters.

In a sense Billy Murray's a fortunate man. On graduation from the United States Merchant Marine Academy he'd been assigned to duty as a marine engineer on an ammunition ship plying Vietnam waters. Defying the tendency of the young to squander money, Billy had used the lucrative income associated with wartime waters toward the purchase of a lovely home in the Mill Basin section of Brooklyn.

Being a handy person, Billy has finished his basement using a nautical motif. Anything and everything associated with a vessel at sea is present. Adding to the museum-like atmosphere are the antique firearms Murray collects as a hobby and as an investment. Since no Super Bowl Sunday is complete without beer, and since the average firefighter is a child at heart, these particular occasions often resemble a scene from "Captain Blood." Mingled with those truly interested in the spectacle being presented on the screen are others more intent at hacking away at one another with the variety of ancient swords that are part of Murray's collection. Naturally, grown men will be pointing guns and screaming "bang, bang, you're dead!" Later, as Murray himself enters into the spirit of the occasion, some of the guns will be loaded and a portion of the neighborhood properly terrorized.

Maureen and Murray's son and daughter are long gone prior to the arrival of the first reveler. Maureen spends the day in the company of a coterie of similarly suffering females. The kids are left with Billy's mother. Billy's mother is precisely where Pudgy Dunn would prefer Billy's dad spend the day. There's a feud of some standing between the pair. The elder Murray had retired from Engine 58. In the process of his stay at that Harlem unit, Lieutenant Murray had entered into a rather senseless dispute with Pudgy. Unaware of the lieutenant's presence, Pudgy one night commented upon the man's advancing years: "Lieutenant Murray has degenerated to the point where his semi-annual erection is now his annual semi-erection!" The outraged Murray had descended on Pudgy like a ton of bricks. It was Pudgy's contention that he'd shined so many poles that he was now allergic to "brass fucking polish."

There's a dog at the Murray residence—a magnificent Irish setter called Ryan. Old man Murray and the dog are pals. Since the elder Murray is seldom enchanted by Pudgy's presence, neither is the dog. On one occasion Pudgy, contemplating paying his share of the day's activities, had laid out the contents of his wallet on a nearby table. Four ten dollar bills and a roll of postage stamps had been promptly swallowed by Ryan. In his outrage Pudgy had kicked in Ryan's direction. The resultant removal of half of one of the legs of Pudgy's pants had been regarded as hilarious by the senior Murray.

Pudgy is not the only member Harry Murray makes nervous. The man doesn't drink and the continuous shaking of his head as he contemplates the reactions of the imbibers is nerve-wracking. Gillian in particular is upset by such puritanical conduct. "I don't give a shit if he is Billy's dad! If he's not gentleman enough to drink with the rest of us, he should be barred!"

Failure to imbibe is not the only shortcoming attributed to this retired lieutenant. Roger Brennan finds him particularly annoying. The older Murray's demands that Roger and the new guy, Jack McBride, get off their asses and assist Silensa in the kitchen, Brennan regards as insulting. Roger's rationale is simple: "This world would be a far better place without old guys!"

There is another annoying habit associated with the old lieutenant. On each and every one of these occasions he has won the rather sizable pool held in conjunction with the game. Normally the winner of any fire department venture throws back a portion of his winnings towards the purchase of another keg of beer. Not Harry Murray. Counting his loot, an obviously conscious effort to make sure it's all there, he leaves with an admonition for his son: "Billy, try your best to stay out of jail!"

The end of the game is usually occasion for serving the meal. Since the elder Murray has left the premises, it's also time for serious revelry. On a particular Super Bowl Sunday, lobster tails with drawn butter were the entree. Naturally, a trail of drawn butter and lobster fragments littered the premises. One of Billy's minor-sized cannons had been hauled into the rear yard and primed. Someone—strongly suspected to be Fitzmaurice—had added a small stone. The resultant explosion, originally planned for sound effect, stove in the side of Murray's oversized outdoor pool. The cascading flow entering Billy's basement reached a height of five inches.

Maureen's screams of outrage were countered by Murray's contention that she had no sense of humor. She's a patient woman, this victim of football mania. Her patience was totally tested on that infamous evening. She had in mind a shower. Those animals were gone. Tomorrow she'd worry about straightening up. Standing in the bathroom, in the buff, about to step into tub, her shrieks alerted Billy. There wasn't much to worry about—nothing much at all. The slumbering Oscar Ratner, blissfully snoring in the bathtub, was completely harmless. Maureen's charges of cruelty, threats of separation, demands for his resignation from the department, were regarded as ridiculous and outrageous by Billy. What the hell was wrong with the woman? After all, hadn't this been the grandest Super Bowl party of them all?

The Big Apple Marathon is another cause for celebration for these Harlem units. The race, entering its 23rd mile, passes their door. It's no picnic for the runners at this point and assistance of a sort is often asked for and rendered. Many of the marathoners merely have need for restroom facilities. They're there for the asking.

Apparatus is parked on the street for a dual purpose. It facilitates response. It also enables sirens to be blown as passing fire department personnel jog along the route. Some of the fire department runners are class performers completing the course in under three hours. Not so with retired Lieutenant Murray. It takes this old timer some five hours to cover the tortuous route. According to Pudgy Dunn, he competes out of spite.

Word of his passing the various firehouses along the course is telephoned in advance. These Harlem firefighters know exactly when he's due to arrive. Their greeting is tumultuous. Sirens blare, bells ring and a host of encouragement thrown in the veteran's direction. Lieutenant Murray has only one reaction. Looking in Pudgy's direction he raises his left hand with four fingers closed in a fist. The middle finger is extended in international greeting.

The lieutenant's reaction never fails to amaze Silensa. "There's got to be some Sicilian in that man. That's the best Italian salute I've ever seen!"

There are members of these Harlem units who find family oriented affairs boring. The annual family picnic and the dinner dance sponsored once a year to placate carping wives are outstanding examples. The rationale is simple. One can hardly cut loose on occasions of this type. It's Oscar Ratner's considered opinion that wives and kids are entitled to room and board and nothing else. To bolster this rather biased opinion, Oscar appears alone on such occasions. To say he does his damnedest to disrupt the placidity and continuity of proceedings is to state the matter lightly.

Being gregarious by nature, the members of Engine 58 and Ladder 26 invite the members of adjoining units to participate in their family wingdings. Whether the flyers spread around the battalion headed "Come one—come all" really include Chief McCarthy is a matter for conjecture. Nevertheless, he did come to one of these affairs. Whether or not he came to relax or to observe the peasantry is difficult to define. It's a certainty he didn't enjoy himself.

It took Oscar no longer than a half an hour to determine his manner of attack. He was seen whispering to Larry Fitzmaurice's oldest son. Shortly thereafter, this stocky duplicate of his father approached the McCarthy heir. Basically, each kid departed the festivities with something he hadn't possessed at the start of the picnic. Young McCarthy had a fat lip and Fitzmaurice's kid had a ten dollar bill.

Fitzmaurice was beside himself. He didn't know whether to congratulate his son or beat the tar out of him. He compromised by confiscating the prize money. He eased his conscience by assuring himself it was essential to maintain his son's amateur status. Besides, it cut down on expenses for the day.

Oscar didn't hand out any ten dollar bills to disrupt the annual dinner dance. The affair was held at a sumptuous Nassau County motel complex. The festivities were adjacent to the pool area and it was felt this added a certain glamour to the occasion. After fortifying himself with four or five belts of rye, Ratner decided it was time for action. Approaching Roger Brennan and his date, Oscar had thrown this rather lovely creature into the pool. Roger, attempting revenge, grabbed Ratner and wrestled vigorously with him until they both joined Roger's date. Gillian, attempting to lend a hand, had fallen overboard only to be joined by half the assemblage on a voluntary basis.

The arriving Nassau County police officers buttressed the considered opinion of the management concerning leaving *now* and *never* returning.

Given the choice of one day to be struck from the calendar, it's quite possible the upper echelon of the department would eliminate St. Patrick's Day. The day's potential for disaster is evident. Thousands of uniformed firefighters, loose on the town in the mood for celebration, have given many a gray hair to worried superiors.

The impossibility of such a huge parade adhering strictly to schedule is felt to be one of the prime causes of early holiday enthusiasm. New York City is usually cold in March and that's excuse enough for early arriving firefighters to fortify themselves against the possibility of pneumonia. One could hardly expect a man to hang around a drafty midtown street twiddling his thumbs. The rationale of the firefighter is simple. Start the goddamned parade on time or face the consequences. Some in official positions are positive that the bars and grilles in the area are responsible for the developing conditions. The contention that *someone* in authority is reached for the purpose of causing delay is regarded as ridiculous by most. There are those who point to the fact that these bars are out of supplies in the space of three hours.

There are organizations in this parade adhering strictly to military discipline. The firefighters, arm in arm, loudly singing out "Harrigan, Harrigan That's Me" are possibly the least disciplined group participating. It's fun and games as far as they're concerned. This attitude has resulted in steps being taken.

The realization that beer in large quantities will be consumed in any event has resulted in the holding of a gigantic get-together in a National Guard Armory. It's felt that corraling the group and confining them to one place might negate the overall potential for disaster. The rationale is correct. Over the years encouraging the men to party in this single spot rather than scattered all over town has cut down on harebrained incidents involving firefighters. It has not cut down on lunacy in the hall itself.

The Holy Name Society picks up the tab for the voluminous quantity of hot dogs, rolls, mustard and, most of all, kegs of beer. Annually the heads of this organization mull over just what absurdity will culminate this year's event. They're never disappointed. Someone always comes through. There is always one man designated "Buffoon of the Year."

On a particular occasion a group of nurses had entered the hall and joined the festivities. The hall was packed. The noise of thousands of firefighters cutting up old touches was almost deafening. On the dais the president of the Society, pleading for order, managed to introduce the Chaplain, the Chief of Department, and the Fire Commissioner himself. Whatever the commissioner had in mind was never delivered. Two figures—both stark naked, both with a paper bag complete with eye slits over their heads—dashed across the dais and into the audience. The joint was being streaked.

It is fair to assume that one of the streakers was a member of the department. The other was not. Later Oscar Ratner was heard to say, "That dame had the finest set of lung warts I've seen in months!"

The commissioner was wild with anger. Grabbing the microphone he'd shouted, "Get me that man and I'll dismiss him from this department on the spot!"

The culprits were out of the door, up the block and into a waiting car in moments. Naturally there was conjecture concerning their identities. Most guesses were wildly speculative and far from the mark. It was the ever observant Pudgy Dunn who hit the nail on the head. "I can't place the dame but there's only one man in the job with that build and that type of red pubic hair. That numbskull streaking the joint was Roger Fucking Brennan!"—a charge vigorously denied by Roger and countered by Gillian's observation that Brennan hasn't told the truth since his discharge from the armed forces.

Quiet Evening In Harlem

Surely the most ardent devotee of fun and games would have to admit that even in Harlem—even for the members of the Fire Factory—there would have to be an occasional "Quiet Evening," a night free of the raucous activity usually associated with the area, an evening free of the sound of sirens, pistol shots, screams, hysteria—an evening devoted to what would pass for normalcy in another area. This is such an evening.

It's nine-fifteen on this Thursday evening in Harlem and Captain Ray Cullen sits at his office desk and stares at the wall. He's deeply disturbed and with reason. For two and a half hours he's polished off the clerical work by banging away at the typewriter and now the outgoing basket is full. The source of Cullen's concern is that the basket is filled with a lot of nonsense.

The units haven't turned a wheel since 6:00 p.m. roll call and while certainly such a lack of activity gives him time for thought, his current mood is one of long standing. He's now positive that he's seen the best of the years in this job. The fun days are over. There had been a time when he'd looked forward to coming to work at this firehouse, but not anymore.

Bitterly, he holds one of the latest communiques from downtown. Once again the constant repetition concerning the prohibition of alcoholic beverages in quarters. Not that he'd ever sponsored a "Night Club"—not that at all. He'd run his company in an adult fashion. His guys toed the mark, behaved like gentlemen and were the most dedicated professionals he'd ever encountered. Now he's supposed to go around sniffing breaths. He'd be damned if he'd do it. He'd pack in the job first. He's made up his mind. Whether he's ready for civilian life or not, he'll put in his retirement papers if this nonsense continues.

Ray walks towards the office window and gazes out at the huge harvest moon hanging over Harlem. At roll call Fitzmaurice had predicted a rash of false alarms. "With a moon like this, every fucking nut in the area will be out pulling boxes!" Fitzie's nuts have yet to make an appearance.

As he stands at the window, the captain is perplexed. How the administration plans on keeping experienced men in the ghetto area puzzles Cullen. For years he's worked at making an assignment to Ladder 26 a pleasurable experience. He's run study classes, attended every off-duty function as one of the boys, did his damnedest to make the atmosphere desirable. He's made Ladder 26 a place a man could look forward to and now this.

Admittedly, he has permitted a small amount of surreptitious drinking. Anytime his platoon returns from a heavy worker he breaks out the bottle of scotch and toasts their health. Where was the harm? That's what he'd like to know. Where was the harm? Not one of his troops had ever abused the privilege and now this asshole Chief McCarthy informs him that this latest directive will be enforced down to the last semicolon and comma.

The captain is sure of one thing. He's sure the administration seems to be concentrating on maintaining a bunch of characters in cushy berths. Every night a new set of directives arrives and each new set seems aimed at keeping these people busy. Cullen never ceases to be amazed that some of the epistles are contradictory in nature. He wonders how a man studying for promotion can keep up with this river of nonsense. Youngsters like Murray and Gillian, both serious students, must surely be over the barrel in their attempts to surmount this never ending flow of hogwash.

What bothers Cullen is the certain knowledge that many of the personnel now issuing restrictive directives had themselves been party boys. A few of them had been something less than excellent firefighters, and this fact increases Cullen's bitterness. The knowledge that martinet discipline will result in the loss of a large part of his personnel concerns Cullen. He's aware that no man in his right mind will travel for hours to reach Chief McCarthy and his witch hunters.

The possibility of transferring out of his present assignment has, of course, occurred to Cullen. It's a move that's rejected out of hand. Ladder 26 is his assignment, his love and his life. He looks out of the window staring into space and seeing nothing. He finally makes up his mind. He feels there's only one way out. Slowly he reaches into the desk drawer and pulls out several letterheads and a few pieces of carbon paper. He inserts them into the typewriter and stares at them for a full five minutes before heading up his report.

The document will be addressed to the Fire Commissioner and will contain a variety of pertinent information concerning Captain Raymond Cullen of Ladder 26. Into this one-page report will be condensed statistics associated with a man who has rescued four human beings and has been cited eleven times for gallantry above and beyond the call of duty. It will be the captain's application for retirement. A triumph for bureaucracy. A tragic loss for the Harlem community.

Lieutenant Anderson is restless tonight. The pile of reports lying on his desk hasn't been touched. Silently he stands at the office window of Engine 58 and stares at the huge yellow moon hanging over the area. He's feeling low and it's the moon that's got him down. Not the moon itself, of course, just its present size and shape.

A beautiful yellow moon always puts him in a blue mood, and with reason. That's the way it was on that June night in 1943 before he shipped overseas. It was the last night he'd spent with Jenny. He's compelled to question his sanity by the fact that a man pushing sixty could still get the blues over a lost love. What's wrong with him? Why can't he ever forget? Surely, he should have gotten over a beautiful teenaged girl who'd had a change of heart. Others had. He certainly wasn't the only guy in his outfit to receive a "Dear John" letter.

What a night it had been. He can recall the ride on the old

125th Street ferry. He'd been in uniform and they'd held hands at the front of the old lumbering boat and stared at the fabulously lighted Palisades Amusement Park. The ferry's been out of service for years and the park's a housing development and still he carries this torch.

They'd swum in that marvelous salt water pool, hit every ride in the area, danced for hours, come back on the last ferry and pledged an eternal and everlasting love. Jenny was all for getting married but he'd played it safe. Why burden a young girl with a possible battlefield casualty?

The letters arrived on an almost daily basis while he was stationed in England. They were all amorous in nature and all anxious for his safe return. Once his outfit hit the beach on D Day he hadn't expected much in the way of mail. After all, there was a war going on. He wasn't disappointed. The mail stopped. His unit slugged its way clear into Germany, leaving a lot of good people behind before he received the news. It seems she'd met a defense worker.

In his rage he'd sworn to kill the guy or at least to beat the hell out of him. When he'd finally met the man, he had to admit he was a pretty decent person. He saw Jenny over the years and on one occasion she'd contacted him directly. Apparently there'd been a bit of family trouble and there was a strong hint concerning the resumption of relations.

While there'd been times when he kicked himself for turning down the offer, his natural reluctance towards breaking up another man's home was just too powerful. It simply wouldn't have worked out. It shortly became all too obvious that she'd made up with her husband. A set of twins too obvious.

The lieutenant thinks of all the guys in the job who are so sure his bachelor life is the grandest one of all. He'd change places with any of them. He realizes all too well he certainly hasn't been celibate. There'd been a never-ending series of relationships ranging from semipermanent to one-night stands. None of them were called Jenny.

Slowly the lieutenant leaves the window and approaches his desk. He picks up the first piece of correspondence and peruses it carefully. He's not amazed that the contents include a warning against alcohol in quarters. Neither is he amazed by the postscript of Chief McCarthy.

Now that he's read the memo, Anderson becomes aware of a pressing need and approaches his locker. Standing on tiptoe he reaches into the upper shelf and comes down with a quart of Chivas Regal. Slowly he pours himself a healthy belt and holds it on high. Walking towards the window he looks up at the moon and offers a silent toast: "Here's to you, moon, and that Boy Scout Chief McCarthy, and Directive 42, but most of all, here's to Jenny."

It has long been apparent that Billy Murray is a creature of habit. This "Quiet Evening in Harlem" will show little variance in pattern. Predictably, he'd worked out with Willie Burrell for an hour in the firehouse basement. His throwing and blocking a variety of kicks and punches would be guaranteed to put his mother into a state of shock if she'd been privileged to witness the exhibition.

He'd showered and, of course, had been in on the meal and he also broke Silensa's chops in the process. He's not troubled at all that he'd lied outrageously while describing the allegedly sumptuous meals served at the United States Merchant Marine Academy. The ambiguity of mentioning "Slatterys' Slop" in the same breath with John's acknowledged culinary artistry fails to disturb his conscience.

Oscar Ratner hadn't been the least bit surprised to be relieved on watch early. Murray's habits are predictable as he finds the housewatch area an excellent place to study. Study comes naturally to Murray or to anyone else who graduated from that tightly run ship known as Kings Point. There's only one way out of that Federal Academy which is so vividly described by its cadets as "the Zoo." One sticks one's nose into a book as a plebe and doesn't remove it for the four-year period leading to graduation.

He'll spend the time on watch perusing a chapter of *Crosby, Fisk and Foster* dealing with the potential hazards associated with a variety of chemicals. If all goes well, he'll have mastered the intricacies associated with extinguishing fires in a variety of chemical solvents.

It's all a matter of priorities as far as Murray's concerned. If an alarm hits in, he'll be treated to the reality of smoke, heat and fire in some tenement hallway. Since Murray's a very practical man, he fully realizes the improbability of an examiner concerning himself with the realities of such mundane situations. He'd therefore prefer to beat the hell out of *Crosby, Fisk and Foster*. Besides, it'll be far less taxing physically. A very practical man, Fireman Murray—a very practical man.

For a full hour, Larry Fitzmaurice has been sitting in front of his locker and going over a pile of bills. It's not the first time that he's aware of the utter impossibility of supporting a wife and seven kids on a firefighter's pay. The fact that his wife will shortly deliver their eighth child fails to ease his tension.

How to meet these obligations? That's the problem. Who to pay and who to let slide? How to balance an unmanageable budget? How to pull money out of thin air? That's the question.

He's tried so hard. He's moonlighted a number of outside jobs but always remains on the razor's edge of bankruptcy. He knows there's criticism concerning the size of his family. To hell with the criticism. He loves those kids.

Silently, he considers the possibility of cashing in one or more of his insurance policies. The risk, of course, will be great. This is a dangerous job. There's none more hazardous. He'll have to think over such a move very carefully. Very, very carefully.

As he sits at the table in the kitchen, John Silensa is planning tomorrow's meal. It was evident that the crew had been inclined to favor the veal parmesan he served this evening. There wasn't even the shred of a leftover. The only criticism had come from Billy Murray. Somehow John gets the distinct impression that this guy had been bullshitting insofar as his description of Kings Point meals is concerned. How the government could afford to stuff several thousand cadets with the type of food described by Murray puzzles Silensa.

There's no doubt in Silensa's mind at all. Murray had to be lying about those meals. Tomorrow he'll serve these animals spaghetti and meatballs with a few sausages thrown in and if that doesn't satisfy Billy Murray, then Billy Murray can go and fuck himself.

For the fifth time in the space of an hour, Oscar Ratner has tried unsuccessfully to put the bite on Pudgy Dunn for the loan of twenty until payday. "How many times do I have to tell you, *no way*? What do you think I am, a million-fucking-aire?"

It's three a.m. and the guy leaving the Acey-Deucy Bar staggers toward the fire alarm box at Fifth Avenue and 117th Street. He's intent on transmitting the same false alarm he's turned in every night this week. His attention is diverted as he looks up at the huge moon overhead and becomes absorbed in its splendor. He reaches into his coat pocket for a book of matches, lights a cigarette and raucously sings "Moon Over Miami!" He staggers north on Fifth Avenue and for the first time in months the guys at the Fire Factory haven't turned a wheel. Of course, they still have six hours to go before the 9:00 a.m. roll call. If they're lucky, they'll stay inside for the balance of the tour. If they're lucky.

The Street Kid

Harlem isn't always quiet; most of the time it's the scene of great activity. Of course, not all of the area's boisterousness is associated with firefighting. Harlem is a big place, a municipality within a municipality. To some people, Harlem is the entire world. Randolph Roberts lives in the area and he's one person who truly understands the meaning of the expression "Harlem USA."

If Randolph Roberts had known his mother, it's possible he might have questioned her concerning his highly improbable first name. Born at the Harlem Hospital on October 2nd, 1968, and promptly deposited with his maternal grandmother, he's known to his peers as Randy. It has, of course, occurred to Randy that he's illegitimate. After all, he's no dummy. The fact that his maternal grandmother's family name is also Roberts strongly implies the lack of male parental responsibility. Tall for his years, Randy is lean and wiry and as black as any native African. For a while he affected an Afro and this was much to his grandmother's dismay. The Afro's gone now—proof that the toughest of Harlem street kids can be bullied into submission by a white-haired grandmother.

Harlem is all this street child has ever known. The farthest south he's been is Central Park. The northernmost perimeter of his worldly experience ends at 155th Street. The only home Randy knows is the East 117th Street apartment presided over by his grandmother. Two flights up and to the rear, the three rooms shared by this pair are typical of the locale. These people take for granted that the apartment is blazing hot in the summer and frightfully cold during the winter. It's the only environment they've ever known. Roaches and bedbugs by the thousands and rats by the hundreds are the norm. Poverty is king on this street. The variety of attempts to circumvent it leave little to the imagination.

Policy is big on the block. Everyone plays the numbers. The dream of a fast buck drains thousands of dollars from an area barely capable of feeding itself. Prostitution gets a big play. Dozens of women grind out a buck hitting the bricks. These working girls are undoubtedly concerned that most of their hard earned money winds up in the pockets of a variety of pimps. It certainly concerns no one else on East 117th Street. The area is a wholesale drug market. Motown Freddie's industrious crew push a diverse selection of lethal products ranging from marijuana to angel dust and touching all the bases in between.

Randy's experimented with a few of Freddie's products. Considering his environment, it would be difficult imagining him *not* becoming involved. His attempts at attaining a high via marijuana have been non-productive. The weed gives him a headache. He skin-popped heroin but abandoned that form of poison when one of his friends mainlined. Leroy had been this kid's name. Leroy overdosed at age fourteen and this had scared the living daylights out of Randy.

Not that his narcotic associations had ended; quite the reverse. He entered the more productive aspects of this business. As a student at Junior High School 120 he'd decided to try his hand as an entrepreneur. Pushing in the area of the school worked out fine for a while. His sudden affluence and his inability conceal it had been his undoing. His sporting a new pair of designer jeans and an equally expensive pair of Adidas had caught his grandmother's attention. Never one to mince words, she'd used a broomstick handle with sufficient effectiveness to terminate Randy's activities in the world of commercial endeavor.

Now certainly there are grandmotherly admirers of Motown Freddie in the vicinity of East 117th Street more than willing to encourage an enterprising youngster. Mrs. Adelaide Roberts, however, is not one of them. She's an ardent disciple of the Risen Lord and attends services held at the Baptist Church on 116th Street. She does not attend these services out of any desire to be seen. She truly believes.

Having lost a daughter to the streets, this good woman has no intention of sending her grandson in the same direction. As far as she's concerned, there's a battle going on. She and Satan will wrestle over the soul of Randolph Roberts. For better or worse, the unsuspecting Randy is in for a hard time.

In an ordinary environment, it's possible Mrs. Roberts would have worked through the school system in her attempts to get her grandson straightened out. Since she's a functional illiterate and barely capable of writing, her relationship with the school system is marginal at best.

Randy's far from stupid. He possesses an inordinate amount of street smarts and his ambitions lead in the directions normally shunned by those seeking academic prowess. The fast buck interests this kid. Sleek cars, alligator shoes, diamond pinkie rings and flashy clothes impress him. More than anything else, he's impressed by the physical prowess of Motown Freddie's main man. George is the name of this headbuster. George is the one who keeps things cool on East 117th Street. Get out of line and George breaks your head.

George is a bad dude—six-five, 265 and not an ounce of fat. Get smart with one of the pushers and George will be all over you. George has a gun. Everyone knows that. He's got a knife, too. More than anything else, he's got a pair of hamlike fists that have sent dozens to the hospitals serving the Harlem community. If Randy has any current ambition, it's to be like George. The thought of being capable of handling street problems in George's inimitable fashion intrigues this Harlem kid.

Being a functional illiterate does not make Mrs. Roberts a stupid person. Not being able to read the editorial section of *The New York Times* is one thing; being blind is another. This basically good, decent woman is frightened. She's terribly concerned for Randy. She realizes that nagging will get her no place, and so she's embarked on a campaign designed to put Randy on the straight and narrow.

Mrs. Roberts will not go near the police department. She

regards that as a waste of time. Nor will she appeal to Motown Freddie. That would be the height of futility. Speaking to her minister would be even more ineffective. That gentle man would have no impression on Randy or any of the other street kids. She has, however, come up with a solution —one that will solve her problem. She's decided to pray. It's as simple as that. If she prays hard enough, the Lord will hear her prayer and set Randolph on the proper path.

Go ahead and laugh if you want to. Mrs. Roberts won't mind. God *will* answer her prayer.

It has, of course, never occurred to Willie Burrell that he might be selected as an instrument of the Lord. Being a firefighter is career enough for Willie. Saving souls is another matter. His adventure as a missionary began in a mundane enough fashion. He agreed to exchange tours with Tim Connelly of Engine 58. Failure to enter into this agreement would have kept him away from 117th Street and away from Randolph Roberts since that street is a considerable distance from any area usually inspected by the members of Ladder 26.

Normal firehouse routine finds Willie Burrell completing any assigned committee work chores as rapidly as possible. There's a method in Willie's haste. On most mornings he adjourns to the basement for a karate workout with his friend Billy Murray. Since there's no one even remotely interested in the martial arts on this particular platoon, Willie occupied himself with the sports section of *The Daily News*. The rather dismal account of the football ineptitude of the Jets left him far from enthused.

He was even less enthused on being summoned to the engine company office. Seemingly, Lieutenant Flannagan, presiding over this platoon, had received notice regarding a leaking fire hydrant on East 117th Street. Willie was to inspect the hydrant and report on its condition.

Given the choice there is simply no way Willie Burrell would have anything to do with East 117th Street. Willie regards the area as a pesthole that is best avoided. As he leaves quarters attired in work clothes and fireman's cap, Willie is just about the most improbable missionary one could imagine. Turning right on Fifth Avenue Willie entered 117th

Street with one thought in mind. He will use his hydrant wrench to test the hydrant and get the hell back to quarters as rapidly as possible. Mrs. Roberts and the Lord have other thoughts on the matter.

On most mornings Geechie Williams, the little punk pushing Motown Freddie's products in this particular section of the block, would have been handling sales in a local hallway. For some unaccountable reason he'd moved his activities near the leaking hydrant in front of the tenement numbered seventeen. Naturally there was a crowd shoving cash at Geechie in exchange for a variety of glassine envelopes.

Totally devoid of physical strength and somewhat lacking in courage, Geechie will never be able to explain his adamant refusal to move from the vicinity of that hydrant. Nor will Willie be able to rationalize his own actions. Picking this flyweight up and tossing him into the middle of the gutter is simply not Willie's style. The fact that Motown's merchandise had scattered to the four winds to be retrieved free of charge by a variety of scurrying addicts had brought George into the picture. Black Belt and all, Willie had never been up against anyone the size of this cat. As he approached Willie, George's utterances had been brief—"Motherfucker, you on your way to the hospital!"

Spectacular as it all appeared, it hadn't been much of a contest. Willie had promptly kicked George in the crotch, leaving that embarrassed behemoth in the middle of 117th Street grasping the family jewels. A smashing blow to the side of George's concrete-like head had leveled him completely. Willie nonchalantly finished his hydrant inspection and proceeded toward Fifth Avenue. He was followed by the admiring Randolph Roberts who had witnessed the entire event.

Randolph had accompanied Willie to the firehouse and had embarrassed him with a host of questions. At a later date Willie had confided in Billy Murray. "Man, I don't know what the hell I'm gonna do with that Randy kid from East 117th Street. First he's bugging the hell out of me about being a fireman. Now he wants karate lessons!"

Try as he may, there's no way Willie will get rid of this kid.

He *will* take him to the 135th Street YMCA for karate lessons. He *will* induce him to hit the books at school. He *will* inspire him to keep himself clean both mentally and physically.

Willie has no choice. Mrs. Roberts has prayed to the Lord and the Lord works in mysterious ways. *Hallelujah and Amen.*

Another Quiet Evening

Mrs. Roberts and her prayers may or may not have resulted in still another Quiet Harlem Evening. Who can tell? God does work in mysterious ways. Maybe this particular night is God's way of saying thanks to Willie. Who's to know? Who can really tell? In any event, God couldn't have picked a better evening to keep the men inside of the firehouse. It's miserable out there. It's snowing and snowing heavily.

The snow is not unexpected. For two days reports of accumulations varying from one to two inches had been predicted. Now at 10:00 p.m. the reaction to the twelve-inch blanket carpeting the metropolitan area is best expressed by Gillian: "That fucking Channel Seven and its idiot forecaster!"

Lack of patience with inaccurate predictions is hardly limited to Jim. The entire city has been caught in the grip of this silent white carpet. The sanitation department, usually on top of conditions requiring plows, wages a losing battle. Stalled cars block a host of intersections. Emergency vehicles find traffic impossible. Pedestrians stagger along slipping, sliding and cursing life in New York City.

The potential for disaster is monumental. Apparatus response time will increase dramatically. Hydrant location will remain a mystery. Sanitation personnel desperately plowing to open up roadways will cover hydrants faster than fire department crews can dig them out. Fire duty is heavy throughout the city. There's a fourth alarm on the West Side waterfront just off 18th Street near the partially demolished West Side Highway. A third alarm occupies the forces assigned to the Astoria area in Queens. Two second alarms in Brooklyn, a host of All Hands jobs throughout the five boroughs and a myriad of minor alarms shifting apparatus from locale to locale occupy the distraught dispatchers.

Here in Harlem, Engine 58 and Ladder 26 haven't turned a wheel. It's as if someone had waved a wand cutting off the area from the rest of the city. The usually dingy neighborhood is strangely beautiful. The large flakes floating lazily down create a Currier and Ives fantasy. An illusion is offered and the uninitiated might feel that here a mugging, a rape, a drug sale, or a devastating fire had never occurred.

Officer personnel have anticipated the worst and have moved to cover all bases. Skid chains have been placed on apparatus. Extra shovels to assist in digging out hydrants are on board. Every member has been cautioned concerning protecting themselves with adequate clothing. Silensa has risen to the occasion and reached the heights in culinary art. He's prepared a bouillabaisse, a stew containing a variety of fish, tomatoes, saffron and other spices. There's plenty of it and it's excellent. John, however, is not in a good mood. He'd dished out the meal with an admonition. "First son-of-a-bitch makes a crack about smells or prices gets whacked right in the fucking mouth!" There had been no remarks.

Chief McCarthy had been in and his attitude suggests that the weather results from shortcomings on the part of the members of these ghetto units. His pique may well have resulted from Silensa's attitude concerning the setting of another place. "There's not enough," was all he'd say to the chief. Privately, he expressed an unwillingness to "cook for any pricks!" His attitude has been heartily endorsed. Fitzmaurice, on his fourth helping, has a comment. "Too bad we didn't have any jalap handy. We could have slipped the bastard a mickey!"

Whether McCarthy's subsequent orders were based on his failure to be served by Silensa is open to conjecture. He wanted personnel outside shoveling snow. He wanted people on hydrant patrol and he wanted them out right away.

Seated at the housewatch desk, snug as a bug in a rug, Roger Brennan feels all is right with the world. His stomach is full. The bouillabaisse had been sensational. The radiator, pleasantly hissing, creates an atmosphere of warmth sufficient to remind him of warmer, softer moments. Last night's chick will have to be revisited.

The freckle-faced Roger yawns, stretches and debates opening up the paperback he's borrowed from Alcock. So far, he finds the thing boring. He tries to imagine how the book sold over a million copies. Roger's sure of one thing. He's going to enjoy this watch. The prospects of sitting on his duff while the less fortunate freeze their butts shoveling snow delights him. It does not delight him for long.

Lieutenant Anderson has arrived and he's accompanied by Bernie Schwartz. Roger is puzzled and wonders what the hell is going on. The lieutenant, hardly the man to keep a person in suspense, informs Roger he's been relieved from housewatch duty. Apparently the lieutenant has a theory concerning shoveling snow. Where practicable, guys over forty will not push the stuff around—and certainly not when young studs are available.

Bernie is embarrassed and he'd rather not create an issue. Roger is outraged. He's sufficiently incensed to actually question Anderson's authority.

"What kind of bullshit is this? I'm the guy on watch!"

"You were the guy on watch! Now you're the guy who's going to change his clothes and get his ass out onto the street shoveling snow!"

"I'm not!"

"You are!"

"I'll call the fuckin' union! I'll make a grievance!"

"Call the Pope! Call the Marines! Call the fucking Mayor! Just make sure you have your ass out on that street within five minutes!"

While he wasn't out on the street in five minutes, Roger did make it in ten. Anderson, hardly enthused by Brennan's minor revolt, was sufficiently annoyed to stay on his tail until Roger was through the door. The white, unmarked, truly beautiful expanse of snow fails to enthuse Brennan. Roger sullenly pilots the shovel and contemplates the scourge of age and authority.

"Old guys," Roger fumes, "Always fucking old guys." If it isn't one old bastard giving him the shaft, it's another. His father with his constant complaints about Roger getting married and that bastard of a platoon sergeant in Nam. Roger recalls old man O'Reilly and his threats. "Stay away from my daughter, you red-headed bastard, or I'll get a gun and blow your balls off!" Not that O'Reilly's daughter had been any great bargain. It was the principle of the thing. After all, he hadn't raped the girl. Just another example of the injustices heaped on his head by senior citizens. Not that he intends to take this current matter lying down. Roger will definitely not take Anderson's outrage without striking back. He has plans for vengeance, plans that will be put in operation before this tour is over.

Roger digs into the snow with enthusiasm. Roger looks further up the block and sees Pudgy Dunn slowly pushing a pile of snow disgustedly away from the firehouse. Willie Burrell accomplishes the same boring feat in another location. One more hour is all Roger needs. One more hour and he'll hit Lieutenant Anderson right where he lives. Roger feels so good he starts to hum. He's actually enjoying himself. Just the anticipation of getting back at Anderson stirs his blood. Nothing sweeter than revenge is Roger's opinion. Absolutely nothing sweeter than revenge.

To say that Pudgy Dunn is unenthused at the prospect of shoveling snow is to put the matter lightly. This new captain's insistence on using matters of this sort to settle minor disciplinary matters Pudgy finds aggravating. Just let the captain try using the goddamned FDR Drive and see how many times he arrives on time. Basically, Pudgy would rather face charges than take the ribbing the men hand out over these matters. Here he is a guy about to be promoted to the rank of lieutenant and the captain treats him like a proby. It's enough to drive a man insane.

Pudgy looks in Willie Burrell's direction. Willie's also feeling the wrath of the captain. Something to do with that idiot karate Burrell and Murray are always working on down in the cellar. Now *that* Pudgy can rationalize. Stopping two guys from committing mayhem makes sense. Getting upset because a man gets caught in traffic is ridiculous. It's enough to drive a man stark fucking crazy. Pudgy looks north towards Brennan. That friggin' yo-yo is actually singing. Pudgy finds it hard to imagine a man being happy about shoveling snow. Sometimes Pudgy wonders just what makes that guy tick. Brennan is, without the slightest shadow of a doubt, the hairiest son-of-a-bitch Pudgy has encountered. Pudgy is puzzled. The last time he looked, Brennan had been on watch. Now the guy's out here shoveling snow and singing. Pudgy is curious. He'll just have to find out what this is all about. Pushing a shovel, he heads in Brennan's direction. That hairbag bastard is up to something. If there's a reason for being happy enough to sing in the middle of a blizzard, Pudgy intends to be privy to any and all information connected with the matter. He pushes the shovel, passing Burrell without comment. Dunn's curiosity got the better of him. Pudgy's logic is simple. No one sings in the middle of a twelve-inch snowstorm without reason. Not even Brennan.

Under normal circumstances Willie Burrell finds it a pleasure being assigned to the new captain's platoon. The man's a professional and knows his job. Moreover, he's a pleasure to associate with. He's a fine, decent human being. Not tonight, though. Definitely not tonight. Willie is annoyed and as aggravated as he's been in one very long time. The captain's wrong on this particular issue. He's out of order. As usual, Willie and his karate pal Murray had headed for the basement for their workout. Since they're both serious disciples of the martial arts, neither has the slightest desire to harm the other. The accident had been just that—an accident. Murray had been the first to admit his fault in the matter. A simple blow normally parried in routine fashion by a person as adept as Billy had slid through and opened a gash over his left eye. That gash had required four stitches and had caused the commotion. Billy hadn't even wanted a medical leave. As far as Willie is concerned, the matter had been blown out of proportion. All that jive about being one man short during serious weather conditions didn't add up. Murray wouldn't have minded riding with a patch over his eye. The whole matter just didn't make sense.

To be chased out into the snow like a damned probationary man fouling up an assignment was the clincher. "Work off some of your excess energy doing something useful" had been the way the captain phrased the matter. As if staying in shape had no relationship to a job of this type.

As he shovels snow towards the westerly side of Fifth Avenue, Willie has only one consolation. As wrong as the captain is in this matter, Willie recognizes the man's basic fairness. He calls his shots the way he sees them. The man's color blind as far as race is concerned and that's Willie's only solace. That Pudgy Dunn—a man a month or so away from promotion—is also being punished, means nothing to Willie. After all, the guy's late for work as often as he's on time. He should be shoveling snow. Willie should be toasting his butt up against a firehouse radiator.

Willie spots Pudgy trudging past and heading in Roger Brennan's direction. What Brennan is doing here puzzles Willie. Certainly the guy hadn't volunteered for snow shoveling. A hairbag of that type never volunteers. Willie likes Brennan. The guy's good for a few laughs and the man's an excellent firefighter. Willie's sure of one thing about Brennan. The dude's got to be watched in small matters. He'll screw anyone into the ground on minor issues. He's an outstanding example of the Vietnam syndrome. He's a number one man. A man scared in the cauldron eating up persons failing to take care of themselves. Willie is a graduate of the same school. He'd put his year in in Nam and, like Brennan, he'd survived.

Willie looks up at the snow drifting down in huge, wet, fat flakes. The area seems beautiful. The quiet, so still it can almost be heard, is peaceful. Serenity is something sadly lacking in this area. Who should know better than Willie? 119th Street had been home for Burrell. He seldom thinks about the area. He dreams about the place often enough and many of the dreams are nightmares. Willie's a pragmatic individual. He can't control his dreams. His waking thoughts are something else. His mind will not dwell on 119th Street. He won't permit it. Talking with these cats might just help him pass the time.

The three snow shoveling outcasts stand near the firehouse wall whispering conspiratorily. Willie giggles and Pudgy shakes his head in disbelief. Roger waves his arms emphasizing a point. Slowly Brennan inches along the wall towards the window adjoining the housewatch area. The desk is empty. Schwartz is probably back in the kitchen grabbing a cup of coffee. Using his key Roger opens the firehouse door. Furtively, he peers around the darkened apparatus floor. He can hear the sound of the television set in the kitchen. There's the sound of voices raised in anger. Gillian argues loudly with Silensa. Brennan heads upstairs towards the office area.

Both offices are empty. Roger, slipping softly into the Engine office, opens the desk drawer and removes a key. It's the key to Lieutenant Anderson's locker. The ever observant Roger had noted its presence on a previous office visit. It hadn't been the only thing he'd noticed. Opening Anderson's locker, Brennan stands on tiptoes and removes an object from the top shelf. He then silently closes the locker door. He replaces the key and retreats down the stairs to the apparatus floor. Looking slyly around he closes the door and rejoins his fellow outcasts.

Entering the office at 11:30 p.m., Lieutenant Anderson is a reasonably happy man. True, he'd been slightly disconcerted by Brennan's attitude concerning the shoveling of snow. That hadn't lasted long. What the hell, hadn't they managed to stay in quarters despite the weather? And how about that meal? Who could ask for more?

Turning to the window he sees the flakes still drifting lazily down. A truly beautiful sight. He hears sounds. Musical sounds. Sounds of harmony. He catches the lilting tones of "Moonlight Bay!" He has to admit it, they're damned good. Probably a couple of locals that have oiled themselves up to withstand the weather. And that gives the lieutenant an idea.

Opening his locker he stands on tiptoe and reaches towards the upper shelf. He reaches and reaches but finds nothing.

The object of his search is missing. Turning on the office lights he peers intently into the area of the upper shelf. Stepping down from the chair he slowly scratches his head. "Son-of-a-bitch! I could have sworn I had a three-quarters full bottle of Chivas in that locker." He listens to the outside revelers. They've swung into a rollicking version of "Camptown Races." "Son-of-a-bitch! What the fuck could possibly have happened to that bottle?"

The lieutenant stands arms akimbo. He's totally perplexed. "What the hell happened to that scotch?" From the outside the trio of outcasts are into "The Good Old Summertime" followed by a first-rate version of "I Wandered Tonight Through the Fields, Maggie!"

As good as they are, the lieutenant is no longer impressed. "I wish they'd stop that goddamned noise. I can't hear myself think!"

Once again, Anderson climbs the office chair peering deeply into the inner recesses of his locker, but it's all a waste of time. He steps down from the chair. "I'd give a week's pay to find out what happened to that booze!" The choir boys are into "Oh! My Darling, I Love You and I Always Will."

It's too much as far as the lieutenant is concerned. Flinging open the office window about to shout an admonition, he's amazed to spot Brennan flinging an empty bottle down the block. As he stares at the bottle turning over and over prior to disappearing into a pile of snow, Anderson has a thought too terrible to contemplate. "Could they have?" "Would they have?" He makes up his mind. "Nah. No way. They wouldn't have the balls!" Besides, he rationalizes, to hell with the bottle. Look at what a night it is outside and how lucky we've been to remain inside.

Anderson heads out of the office, down the stairs and towards the kitchen firmly convinced that "Somebody up there likes us—that's for sure!"

Mrs. Adelaide Roberts of East 117th Street has reached the same conclusion.

The Party

Firefighters love to party. Anything and everything is cause for celebration. Of course, few department members emulate Brennan, Burrell and Dunn. Drinking a bottle of the lieutenant's scotch in a blinding snowstorm is hardly the norm. Partying, as a rule, takes place in more mundane environments and in a more normal manner.

Tonight's gathering is indicative of the average firefighter's reason for getting together. That no one but firefighters will attend the gathering is not unusual. Firefighters are a rather private group and prefer their own company.

In a society where lasting relationships are regarded as naive, the firefighter stands out as a rare exception. No group is as close knit. Psychiatric evaluation might conclude that shared dangers make such interaction essential. Whatever the reason, men who fight fires prefer their own company. It all has a beginning. Once a man is off probation, he becomes part of an elite group. Since firefighters are far from bashful, the newly appointed man will be made aware that he has been assigned to "the best goddamned company in the finest fire department on the face of the earth!"

To the newly initiated, there are unwritten rules—rules that have been handed down from the days of horse-drawn apparatus. An engine company fighting a fire will never voluntarily surrender its line. Regardless of physical pounding, men assigned a hose line consider it necessary to finish what they start. Standing outside of an involved building and contemplating the realities of another company operating *your* line is a nightmare shared by members of dedicated engine company units. Naturally, similar rules affect firefighters assigned to ladder companies. The area immediately above a fire is a hellhole. The hottest gases, the most vicious and punishing conditions exist at this spot. The area must be searched diligently. Masks have been issued in recent years. Masks make the area above a fire floor tenable, but they also impede vision and make searching difficult. The possibility of missing the kid hiding under the bed often requires the firefighter to violate rules and regulations by removing the facepiece of his mask. His rationale is simple: "Fuck the rules and regulations!" Besides, rules and regulations are promulgated by guys sitting behind desks. Guys sitting behind desks are regarded as pariahs.

Firefighters work together, they bed down in the same bunkroom, they eat the same meals, and on occasion they die together. Since they're that close, it follows that they party together. Fire department celebrations come in many forms, but none more spectacular than the promotion or retirement party. Since both retirement and promotion indicate separation from the unit, the farewell must be as grandiose as possible. Weeks of preparation are involved. A suitable area, large enough to contain a horde of celebrants, will have to be selected. Copious quantities of food and enough beer to float a battleship have to be purchased. Notice must be given to celebrants far and wide, including those retired. To miss such an occasion is simply not done. Suitable mementoes must be selected for those severing their connection with "the best goddamned company in the finest fire department on the face of the earth!" It's all very complex.

The night selected is, of course, a problem. Firehouses never close and someone is on duty every minute of every hour of every day. Usually Pudgy Dunn is faced with the dilemma of selecting the particular day for company rackets. For all the years he's been assigned to this Harlem firehouse, he's been roundly abused. "This is the second friggin' affair in a row I've been working!" "How come you're always off when the rackets are run?" "Got your nose up the captain's ass again, don't you Pudgy?" "I see *he's* off duty the night of the party!" And so forth! And so forth! And so forth!

Pudgy won't be abused this year. Someone else will run the present festivities scheduled by the members of these Harlem units. The reason is simple. Pudgy is one of the guests of honor. He's being promoted to the rank of lieutenant. Along with retiring Captain Cullen and Fireman Ratner, he'll be feted at McCormack's in the Throggs Neck section of the Bronx.

To the uninitiated the selection of a hall miles from the firehouse may seem rather odd. Gillian is in charge of the current affair and has a ready explanation. "Where the hell else would we go?" McCormack's is run by a group of enterprising firefighters. Firemen are great moonlighters and no one battles the inflationary spiral harder. Patronizing an enterprise run by a fellow firefighter hardly requires explanation.

As usual, preparation of food for the two hundred guests is under the supervision of John Silensa. Despite his usual threats to quit, he's secretly happy. At long last he has Gillian precisely where he wants him. "You're so fucking smart with your college education. Let's see what you can do at the supermarket with the amount of money we have to feed this mob!"

The night selected for the festivities is clear and moonlit. One can actually see a few stars; a triumph of sorts in New York City. A person driving towards McCormack's can see the lighted expanse of the Throggs Neck Bridge. The lovely one-family homes in the area represent the last bastion reserved for middle-class residents in an embattled Bronx. This is the way much of the Bronx used to be when Ray Cullen was a boy. Now driving towards McCormack's and his farewell to men he's served with for many years, he's in a contemplative mood. He wonders where the thirty-odd years have gone. It seems only yesterday he'd finished probationary school and now it's all over. It's a sad occasion for this man. He's going to miss the Fire Factory. He wonders if some of the older men will show—Harry Murray, Gene O'Hara, Bert Sweiger. It's always so good to see them and so sad. The ravages of time on men once so strong and so virile is heartbreaking.

Cullen turns right and drives down the block towards

McCormack's and looks for a parking space. As he locks the car, his mind turns back to other, younger days. He doesn't owe a dime and his family's grown. He thinks of all the time he's spent wishing and hoping for debt-free days. Now he'd go back to fourth grade pay, to the small Bronx apartment, and to the lovely young bride and the new baby that seemed to arrive every year.

He looks down the block and there's a crowd standing in front of McCormack's. He spots Oscar Ratner shaking hands with Gene O'Hara. He thinks of the time he's cursed the insane Ratner into hell and out again. He remembers the man's remarkable bulldog courage as a firefighter. Walking towards the group, Cullen recalls one of Oscar's more spectacular escapades. Basically, Cullen acknowledged his own responsibility in the matter. Oscar had purchased a new Chevrolet. Naturally, this had been cause for celebration. The crazy bastard had spent the day drinking and arrived at quarters with half a load. In order to get rid of him, Cullen had assigned him to messenger duty. Oscar'd used his car on the detail and parked it a block from the firehouse. In the morning— forgetting about messenger duty and the reparking of the new Chevrolet—he'd gone into shock. "They've stole my fucking car —they've stole my fucking car!" Naturally, Oscar had reported the apparent theft and naturally the local cops had promised full cooperation. Some five days later Oscar, on the back step of the speeding pumper, had spotted his car precisely where he'd left it on returning from messenger duty. Getting into the car at the end of the tour he'd proceeded home only to be picked up on the Belt Parkway for possessing a stolen vehicle. As a result of the episode Oscar's dislike of police authority had become legendary. Ray walks towards McCormack's with his hand held out. There's a whole lot of friends here—a whole lot of friends. He's beginning to feel a lot better.

Coming off the Brooklyn Bridge and entering the lane serving the northbound approach to the FDR Drive, Pudgy Dunn hopes Larry Fitzmaurice had been joking. The possibility of retired Lieutenant Murray being selected as toastmaster to present the celebrants with their gifts is nightmarish. Now, on his way to McCormack's, Pudgy's made up his mind. He will not approach any dais presided over by Lieutenant Murray. The old bastard would destroy him if presented with such an opportunity.

Cutting over to the right lane, Pudgy hopes Gillian hasn't screwed things up too much. Since he's one of the celebrants, it's only natural Pudgy would appreciate a well-run affair. The years he's assumed responsibility for honoring others makes it imperative that his own party be conducted in an efficient manner. Not that he contemplates everything going right. That would be asking too much. Pudgy's used to being screwed. Nothing ever comes up smelling like roses for Pudgy. His assignment as a newly appointed lieutenant is explanation enough. Bernie Schwartz and his contact downtown are outstanding examples. For weeks Bernie had assured Pudgy that a Harlem lieutenancy was in the bag. Then the reality of that goddamned special order. Pudgy could hardly believe his eyes. "City Fucking Island—the slowest unit in the New York City Fire Department." It was bad enough that the assignment was far from his Brooklyn home. What made it intolerable was the attitude of the guys from Harlem. Every day something else transmitted via department channels. First the Coke bottle containing smoke—in case he'd forget what it looked and smelled like. Next a charred piece of wood, symbolic of the actions of real firefighters. The four Harlem cockroaches described as one bull and three cows ripe for breeding purposes. Enough to drive a man crazy.

Pulling into the center lane Pudgy gets an uneasy feeling. Traffic is slowing to a walk. Turning on his car radio he's in time for the seven o'clock news. The advice of the broadcaster to avoid the FDR Drive is unappreciated. Traffic is at a standstill. Pudgy is now only too aware that he'll be late for his own party. Looking wildly to the right and to the left and turning towards the rear, he knows he's trapped. As far as the eye can see, traffic is at a complete standstill. Finally, he steps from his stranded vehicle, looks towards the sky, and as if in search of divine intervention, he begins to shout:

"I HATE THE FRANKLIN FUCKING DELANO ROOSEVELT DRIVE! I HATE THE FRANKLIN FUCKING DELANO ROOSEVELT DRIVE! I HATE THE FRANKLIN FUCKING DELANO ROOSEVELT DRIVE!"

For a time those in adjoining cars were firmly convinced they'd been trapped in traffic with a raving maniac. Some two minutes later Pudgy was joined by one man, then another and eventually a third. Ten minutes later the resounding shouts of trapped motorists informing the world they hated "THE FRANKLIN FUCKING DELANO ROOSEVELT DRIVE!" could be heard as far north as Gracie Mansion. Whether or not its occupant, Mayor Koch, attached any significance to their complaints is debatable.

Oscar Ratner is reasonably happy as he stands in front of McCormack's and shakes hands with the arriving celebrants. Somehow he's managed to weather the variety of storms stirred by his penchant for creating difficulties. Basically, Oscar realizes he'd been lucky to get out of probationary school—to say nothing of hanging around long enough to collect a pension. Of course, being assigned to Harlem for all of his years in the job had been a help. Officer personnel like Ray Cullen and Frank Anderson were inclined to overlook the peccadilloes of conscientious firefighters, a trait noticeably absent in areas placing emphasis on spit and polish.

Fundamentally, Oscar resents the implication that he might be slightly off his trolley. Personally, he prefers to regard his actions as simple honesty. Telling that prick McCarthy what he'd thought of him required guts as far as Oscar is concerned. It all seemed so basic. How else could McCarthy be made to realize his mistakes if he weren't told about them? It was somewhat the same as the police sergeant in Bridgeport, Connecticut some three years ago. Oscar had refused the drunk-o-meter test because he wasn't drunk. Actually, he'd hardly been drinking at all. Why they'd stopped him had been a mystery to Oscar. When the guy made the crack about drunken firefighters, Oscar had blown his cool. Of course, he'd whacked the cop. The man needed straightening out. He could never understand what all the uproar had been about. Gene O'Hara, as UFA Trustee for the Borough of Manhattan, was the guy who'd bailed him out. And there's good old Gene! What a lifesaver that man had been.

They're entering the hall now. They come in a variety of shapes, sizes, ages, and colors. Men in their seventies and newly appointed kids, barely out of probationary school, have a common bond. They're members of the Fire Factory. Things start off rather slowly. They usually do. There's much handshaking. Older, retired members who haven't seen one another since the last occasion have a lot of catching up to do. Some of the retired men have travelled a considerable distance. Gene O'Hara is up from Florida. Henry Clark, the small dapper black retiree, has flown in from Los Angeles. Distance is nothing to these men. Reliving experiences at the Fire Factory is a *must*. It's something that keeps them alive from one year to the next.

The food is being brought in. Trays and trays of Silensa's delicacies will be served buffet style. The beer's been tapped. A small rolling bar has been set up for those requiring more exotic mixtures. Lieutenant Murray is demanding root beer. He's simply not in the mood for cola. He's mildly disappointed at Pudgy Dunn's absence; the variety of ploys to drive his adversary insane had been well thought out. He finds it hard to believe the guy would miss his own promotion party to avoid conflict. Lieutenant Murray has made up his mind. If Pudgy fails to show, he'll never forgive him. Chickening out of an unpleasant situation will be intolerable and hardly worthy of a member of the Fire Factory! Billy Murray, aware of his dad's feelings, has one thought. Pudgy Dunn had better get his ass up here pronto or face the consequences.

As the tempo picks up, Jim Gillian, major domo for the evening, is becoming aware that it's lonely at the top. In complete charge of arrangements, Jim is close to panic. He's lost the paper listing those who have laid out cash in advance and those who have not. Additionally, he can't remember which suppliers were paid. He's positive he'd taken care of the butcher and has a receipt some place if he could only lay his hands on the goddamned thing. A little cooperation from

Silensa wouldn't hurt. His yelling about the butcher calling John's wife and screaming about the meat bill hardly helped matters. Jim is beginning to wonder how Pudgy Dunn put up with all this bullshit for all these years. Jim sees fit to ignore his being one of Pudgy's prime sources of aggravation.

Things are starting to swing into gear and the noise is deafening. The men split into groups and a variety of topics are under discussion. Billy Murray and Larry Fitzmaurice loudly debate the recent football victory over the police department. It's Billy's contention that Fitzmaurice wasn't going any place without the hit he'd put on the police department's ball carrier. Fitzie has an answer. "It's a damned good thing it wasn't reversed. If you'd caught that fumble they'd have pulled you down from behind. You're slow as shit!"

In one corner of the room Willie Burrell is demonstrating a kata, one of the stylized rituals designed to drum a sense of discipline and order into serious students of the martial arts. He is far from enthused by Oscar Ratner's opinion of katas in general and karate in particular. "Oscar, you're one of the guests of honor here so I'm going to overlook your using the word faggot in association with karate on this occasion. Be cool, Oscar! Enjoy your retirement. Stop breaking my balls, man!"

John Silensa is involved with Harry Alcock. "I don't give a fuck what you think about garlic! I'll use all the garlic I feel like. I'm the cook. If you don't like Italian cooking, get a transfer." Silensa is not in a good mood. He's positive Gillian's got everything screwed up. Additionally, he'd had trouble with Brennan. Roger had flatly refused to assist in unloading Silensa's station wagon. "Get McBride. He's the proby. Let him help with all that food. I'm a Third Grade Fireman now. So, get off my case!" One of the retired men had attempted to be a comedian and that hadn't helped. "No, Captain Regan, there's nothing moving in the rice pudding. Those are raisins, not cockroaches. Just stop being a fucking wise guy. You're out of the job now and I ain't taking any of your bullshit tonight."

Ray Cullen and Harry Murray are attempting harmony

with Frank Anderson. Since Lieutenant Anderson is tone deaf, the results lack the qualities demanded by music appreciators. Nevertheless, they struggle along. Naturally the song praises a part of the area associated with the Fire Factory. Over the years hundreds of responses to that house of horrors grandiosely named "Cadley Hall" had registered on the consciousness of Cullen and Murray and they'd composed a song in honor of the structure and its occupants. It seemed only fitting that the number be called "The Ballad of Cadley Hall." Locked arm in arm, the musically inclined trio sing loudly if not melodiously:

"Oh, Cadley Hall, Oh, Cadley Hall
There are cockroaches in your walls!
And bedbugs in your coaches, too
And you have rats like kangaroos!
Oh, Cadley Hall, Oh, Cadley Hall
There are cockroaches in your walls!"

The first of the numerous verses associated with Cadley Hall naturally attracts attention. Everyone belonging to the Fire Factory has been to Cadley Hall. Half of the assemblage joins in the second chorus.

"You've got your nuts and screwballs, too
Pudgy Dunn lives in apartment two!
Oh, Cadley Hall, Oh, Cadley Hall
There are cockroaches in your walls!"

Mention of Pudgy Dunn brings to mind his startling absence. He'd never missed one of these rackets. It did seem rather odd that he'd miss his own. The third verse is entered into less enthusiastically. Some of the celebrants are becoming concerned.

"Upstairs above in apartment three
For a buck and a quarter you get tiddle-de-dee!
Oh, Cadley Hall, Oh, Cadley Hall
There are cockroaches in your walls!"

It was at this precise moment when Pudgy made his entrance. Mad enough to chew nails, he's an easy target for retired lieutenant Murray. Grabbing the microphone, Murray takes advantage of his opportunity. "And now making his usual late arrival. One of the great assholes of this or any other era.

The City Island Flash. Smokeless Pudgy Dunn!"

Being the perverse creatures they are, these Harlem firefighters must demonstrate their fondness for Pudgy in rather odd fashion. In a normal society such feelings might possibly take the form of an accolade showing their affection. Firemen are not normal. Pudgy must be "himmed." Under the circumstances "himming" is almost traditional. Pointing in Pudgy's direction, every man loudly chants. "Him—Him—Fuck Him!"

As Pudgy vainly attempts to explain the vagaries of the FDR Drive and his abiding hatred for this stretch of road serving Manhattan Island, the party picks up steam. Roger Brennan, an accomplished guitarist, has broken out his instrument. The device, complete with electric amplifiers, creates a remarkably professional impression. He's strumming away to the tune of "Bill Bailey." On the microphone Harry Alcock and Tom Henderson softly harmonize. Henry Clark moves into a soft shoe-shuffle and to his right Willie Burrell breaks into a Harlem strut. Billy Murray, standing on a table, whips out a wide sampling of karate kicks. They're all singing now: "Won't you come home, Bill Bailey! Won't you come home! She moaned the whole night long!" Harry Murray, Gene O'Hare, Ray Cullen and Frank Anderson start a conga line. ". . . I put you out with nothing but a fine tooth comb!" The conga line is the length and breadth of the hall now. Only Gillian and Silensa, arguing loudly as to who fucked up this entire party, abstain.

It would seem rather incongruous that a man with sufficient intelligence to rise to the rank of Battalion Chief would wander uninvited into a situation populated by firefighters who hate his guts. Temporarily detailed as Acting Deputy Chief of Department to this area of the Bronx, Chief McCarthy has decided to check out the affair. The fact that he's on the list for Deputy Chief and will shortly be promoted to that rank may have emboldened him to the point of insanity.

His first action had been directed towards harrassing the personnel of McCormack's with a demand to examine a variety of permits. He seemed visibly disappointed when all was in order. Striding into the area of festivity—a truly handsome figure in his immaculate uniform—he stands aghast at the actions of these barbarians. It was Fitzmaurice who first noticed him. Striding towards the chief, Fitzie had stopped, smartly saluted, about-faced, lowered his trousers and mooned McCarthy. He was shortly joined by three-quarters of the assemblage in what was described by Ray Cullen as the finest collection of assholes he'd ever seen. Throughout the mooning Roger never missed a beat. "Won't you come home, Bill Bailey! Won't you come home! She moaned the whole night long!" McCarthy's departure—amidst a bombardment of rolls directed at the chief as he scurried towards the door—whipped the festivities even higher.

Some two hours later the arriving squad car from the local precinct was parked in front of McCormack's. Police Sergeant McGloin and Patrolman Shapiro entered the festivity and gazed around the room. They found nothing unusual in the actions of the celebrants. They were concerned that Oscar Ratner and Larry Fitzmaurice had chosen to butt heads. They regarded as par for the course that Pudgy Dunn and Harry Murray were arguing violently and calling one another a variety of vile names. The tall black man and his short stocky companion, both bare footed and throwing karate kicks in one another's direction, did concern them momentarily. Since both seemed rather expert, however, the cops decided to leave them alone.

Both officers found the musical expertise of the red-headed kid rather pleasing. The dozen or so close-knit groups, talking, singing, arguing and arm wrestling, seemed rather normal. Proceeding to the buffet the cops made themselves sandwiches and headed out of McCormack's.

The sergeant turned to look at the group and directed a comment towards his subordinate. "Shapiro, I simply can't figure out that asshole Chief McCarthy's beef. This is one of the most orderly firehouse parties I've ever seen. Let's get the hell out of here!"

And so they did, leaving the celebrants to themselves, to create memories, moments to contemplate, enlarge upon and treasure. After all, what is a firefighter—or anyone else for that matter—without his memories.

Requiem for a Fire Company

At times, life in the fire department can be remarkably similar to circumstances in any environment. There are good days and there are bad days. The fire department party held in the Throggs Neck section of the Bronx concerned itself with the joy of living. While the joy of living is certainly a source of great satisfaction, there are other aspects associated with a connection to the Fire Factory. Many are memorable. A few of them are tragic. Some affect every man in the unit; others affect the entire community. Occasionally there is a brief moment when the operations of one firehouse touch the entire city. This is such an occasion.

Bernie Schwartz had been at the party; wild horses couldn't have kept him away. That was last week. Today is another day, an occasion for other problems. Bernie has something on his mind and while it's a situation that might have thrilled another man, Bernie finds the matter annoying.

Actually, Bernie's state of mind has nothing to do with the fire department. It concerns his outside source of income, the moonlighting phase of his working life.

The insurance business is what's on Bernie's mind, the fact that it's too big and his basement too small. Ten years ago his office had been in his hat. Five years ago he paneled the basement, hired a girl and set up a filing system. Now with three girls, six phones and a minimum of space, conditions occasionally approximate a three-ring circus. The number of screwups in the past month have been embarrassing. Of course, his insistence on pursuing a fire department career has something to do with the chaotic office conditions. Crawling down long, nasty, smoke-filled Harlem hallways often makes it impossible for his clerical staff to reach him regarding important decisions. Not that being assigned to Harlem had cost him business; actually the reverse is true. Apprised of Bernie's refusal to open up his files for fire department inspection, the members assigned to this ghetto area have literally forced business his way.

Bernie would like to keep the business right where it is. It's convenient. He can run upstairs for a cup of tea or anything else he might have in mind. It's a lovely home in a lovely neighborhood, but that goddamned basement and that idiot filing system are just too archaic. The business will have to move. He has a few ideas. Some of them are his own. Others have been suggested by his accountant, his attorney and even a few of the guys in the firehouse. He's been playing around with setting up a small computer system and hiring at least one more girl. He's nosed around about office space and naturally some of the sharks have been nipping at his flanks. That meshugga gonif over on East 14th Street had mistaken Bernie for a complete idiot. He gave Bernie a line about Jewish boys sticking together and tried foisting on Bernie a Kings Highway walkup smaller than his current location. That the place had cockroaches was disgusting; that the guy mistook him for an imbecile was annoying.

Bernie has a place in mind. He's put out a few feelers, just enough to let the owner know he's interested. There's a space in a building on Nostrand Avenue near Avenue "T." The place is a former nursing home, is spacious and clean—it's just what he's been looking for. The owners are demanding a one-year lease. Bernie won't buy that. Being put over a barrel in a year's time is not Bernie's idea of a sound business practice. It'll be a long-term lease or nothing. Bernie wasn't born yesterday.

He'll have to do his own redecorating, but that doesn't concern Bernie. There's a host of moonlighting firefighters capable of performing professionally in that area. Anytime Bernie has a dollar to spend, it goes in a firefighter's direction.

Bernie looks at the clock. It's four-fifteen and time to hit the road. He's due at Engine 58 for a six p.m. to nine a.m. tour. He hopes it's a quiet night; he feels a bit tired. Last night was rough. He looks around the basement office and the girls are all busy. Muriel is out shopping and should be back in time to lock up the office. Bernie would feel a lot happier if Muriel were here. It would be nice to kiss her goodbye.

Roger Brennan is positive of two things. If he never sees another beer or another broad again, it will be too soon. Here it is time to hit the road for the firehouse and he's still bleary-eyed and in need of a shave. He'll have to do something about restructuring his life-style. He'll have to establish a few priorities. Getting out of his room and past his mother will be a problem. Holding his aching head in his hands, he's conscious of one of life's realities. Everything has its price. Living at home with one's parents is economically satisfying but one must pay the piper. That gray-haired old lady knows exactly what time he came staggering in. Her lengthy lecture is as inevitable as her attempts to match him up with one of her friend's daughters.

He looks at his watch and it's time to haul ass. He rubs his chin contemplating the possibility of passing up a shave. No way. He has the first watch. It would be just his luck to have that prick McCarthy in for roll call. Roger silently ponders calling the medical office regarding a medical leave. After all, he *is* sick. He's also hungover. The thought of a visiting medical officer finding him in his current condition causes his stomach to do a few nip-ups.

Brennan stands up and staggers towards a mirror. The sight is revolting. How the hell did he let himself get in this condition? He searches for his shoes and finds one. Where the hell is that other one? Could he have come home with one shoe? Fuck it, I'll dig out another pair. He hopes there's an Alka Seltzer in the medicine cabinet. More important, he hopes he can keep it down.

Roger moves away from the mirror, picks up a bathrobe and shoves his feet into his slippers. He hopes the bathroom will be empty. If he can just stand under the shower, he'll feel a lot better. Perhaps this might just be his lucky day. If all goes well, Mom will be out shopping. There might just be time for a shave, a shower, an Alka Seltzer and a cup of coffee. There's not a sound and except for himself the house is empty. Man, this really is his lucky day.

The inevitability of getting himself into situations with his brother-in-law never ceases to amaze Frank Anderson. Once again, he's met his sister and her husband for dinner and once again he wishes he were anyplace but in the company of that klutz. Ellen was always a pretty girl and is still not bad looking for a woman well into her forties. Frank realizes his sister idolizes this asshole. What she sees in the guy confuses Anderson. Why she stays with him remains a mystery.

For the twenty-three years this bird has been married to his sister, Anderson has been used as a patsy. The myriad of loans have turned into outright donations. The money doesn't bother Frank. Ellen is his favorite relative. It's the guy's patronizing attitude that embitters Anderson. It's his attitude of arrant superiority. Anderson's gone away from each and every one of these meetings with the distinct feeling of being used.

It does little to improve Anderson's humor that they're both lieutenants in the fire department and both from the same neighborhood. His brother-in-law never misses an opportunity to rub Frank the wrong way. His detail to headquarters is an outstanding example. His conviction that one would have to be an idiot to serve in Harlem when one has the opportunity to hide behind a desk is galling.

Years back, the guy's outright bragging concerning a wartime assignment as an MP in the Times Square area in contrast to Frank's front line activities had been bothersome. Most annoying had been his habit of referring to Jenny. It was well known in the old neighborhood that Frank had been Dear Johned. Only his brother-in-law makes constant reference to the matter. "Saw Jenny and her husband. She's still a great looking chic. Never saw anyone so wild about her husband!"

Frank looks at his watch and wonders how much he'll be touched for on this occasion. His sister's already informed him that Junior's college tuition is overdue. There'd also been something about Joe's tough luck in the stock market, and the usual song about how hard Joe tries. He wishes he were in the firehouse right now. If ever there's a tour he'll welcome, this will be the one.

"C'mon time, shag ass! I want to get away from here and up to the firehouse so bad I can taste it! This is one tour I can hardly wait for! Anything to get away from this guy. Anything!"

As he speeds along the Taconic Parkway, Jim Gillian once again curses the work chart and all those associated with its creation. He just can't keep the goddamned thing straight in his mind. Of course, he finds it annoying that his wife has no difficulty understanding the bloody thing. Once again, she'd returned from shopping horrified to find Jim perusing Chapter 19 of the Administrative Code. "You're on a forty-eight hour leave of absence, not a seventy-two. You're due in tonight, not tomorrow!"

He just can't afford to be late. As nice a guy as this new captain is, it's well known that he's aggravated with Jim's constant work chart foul-ups. Jim whips past a slow-moving Honda. Hopefully, the friggin' Major Deegan Expressway won't be jammed. This is one tour Jim has no intention of missing. He's going to be on time come hell or high water.

Billy Murray's kissed his wife and kids goodbye, and he's looking forward to this firehouse tour. He has the whole thing planned. He's worked out a wheel kick he'll spring on Willie Burrell. As he drives west on the Belt Parkway he contemplates the timing necessary to suck Willie into falling for such a maneuver. Given the element of surprise, Billy figures he has a chance.

Murray also has plans for the rest of the evening. After supper he'll pick up Bernie Schwartz's watch and go over Chapter 19 with Jim Gillian. There's a couple of items on refrigeration they've both found puzzling. It's best to get them sorted out since the lieutenant's test isn't that far off. Yes, figures Billy, this is one tour that I'm going to put to good use. If I can only put that wheel kick over on Willie, it'll be the start of a tour I'll never forget.

The world is out of its mind as far as John Silensa is concerned. The amount of money he'd laid out for groceries and meat for tonight's meal is unbelievable. That fucking Gillian will be sure to bellow at the top of his lungs. Let him bellow loud enough and it'll be the last meal John cooks in this firehouse. That's right, John assures himself. It just might be the last meal he ever cooks in this firehouse.

Larry Fitzmaurice is annoyed. Six hours tending bar, six hours listening to the problems of a variety of lushes, and now a flat tire. Here it is, five-twenty and he faces three miles of Manhattan rush hour traffic before he reaches the firehouse. He's got to get that goddamned tire on and start moving.

Larry isn't worried about being late. It's just that he doesn't want to take advantage of a nice guy like Lieutenant Anderson. This had been a day to end all days. One damned bar problem after another. First the guy with the hundred dollar bill. The age old bar room racket. Order a drink and then pull the hundred dollar bill bullshit. Naturally, there had to be a tough guy. A day behind the stick in a Manhattan bar wouldn't be complete without some fool flexing his muscles. Of course, the climax had been when the night bartender called in sick. Dragging the owner out of the woodwork so that Larry could head for the firehouse had been a problem.

Fitzmaurice is moving uptown at last. He's bucking the traffic. If only he could spend more time with his wife and kids. The absolute impossibility of making ends meet on a firefighter's salary is heartbreaking. He wonders what Silensa will be serving tonight. What a great bunch of guys! He's in the mood for a good meal. He's really looking forward to the firehouse tonight.

It's 5:50 and he's only a few blocks from the firehouse. He hopes there's a parking space available. There's nothing like a day's bartending to make one appreciate *the job*. This is one night Fitzie will be glad to spend in the firehouse.

Captain Kennedy of Ladder 26 would like to report for duty on one occasion without finding some bizarre suggestion from Battalion Chief McCarthy. Tonight it's hydrants. Ladder 26 will swap rigs with Engine 58. Using the pumper, Kennedy's crew will inspect hydrants from 6:15 p.m. to 9:15 p.m. Alcock will remain with the pumper as Motor Pump Operator. Silensa and Gillian will stay with the hook and ladder as chauffeur and tillerman. Brennan, sporting a ferocious headache, will be detailed to Ladder 26 for the tour.

At six-fifteen Captain Kennedy and his crew left quarters on hydrant inspection. At six-twenty, seven box 1377 hit in for a fire in a six story elevator apartment on 117th Street and Seventh Avenue. Constructed at the turn of the century and occupied by a variety of indigents on welfare assistance of one sort or another, the building is a prime headache for the firefighting forces.

Hardly a week passes without a fire of some sort taking place in this building. Stretching hose up and around the staircase surrounding the elevator is always a problem. Tonight, Anderson's crew, now assigned as a ladder company, will not be faced with that problem. Not that they'll have an easy time. Three rooms in a fifth floor apartment are heavily involved and there's a report of persons trapped in that area.

Getting to the upper part of the building is murder. The narrow, twisting stairway is being used by a horde of tenants fleeing the structure. Lieutenant Anderson has established his game plan. Silensa and Gillian will head for the roof to provide necessary ventilation. They'll also look over the side for persons possibly hanging out of windows looking for help.

Murray and Fitzmaurice will force entry where necessary and search the apartment immediately above the fire. This will be one nasty task. The lieutenant will accompany Bernie Schwartz into the fire apartment. Bernie, equipped with a two-and-a-half gallon pressurized extinguisher, will do his best to cool down the area while Anderson makes a search for the reportedly trapped occupants. It will be no picnic.

Captain Kennedy and his crew had inspected precisely one hydrant when the radio dispatcher had notified them box 1377 had been transmitted. Since they were on Palladin Avenue and East 118th Street, the run west, through dense traffic, would be lengthy.

Turning right on 116th Street and Seventh Avenue, Kennedy can see dense clouds of smoke pushing from the upper floors of a building on the west side of the avenue. He's been here before and he knows they're in for a rough time. The stretch around the elevator shaft will be murderous. The captain notes the raised aerial and he can see Gillian and Silensa heading for the roof. He spots a police car parked directly in front of the hydrant nearest the building. He is outraged. He wonders when these people will learn to stay the hell away from hydrants. He sees a mob of people pushing out from the building and starts to figure how many lengths of hose he'll require for this stretch. He mutters a short prayer, steps down from the apparatus and heads for the involved building.

Pushing up the stairway through the descending group of tenants, Frank Anderson knows he's getting old. His boot-clad legs are tired and he's having trouble breathing. Murray and Fitzmaurice are taking the stairs two at a time, and already they're two flights ahead of him. Anderson has the feeling he'd enjoy riding that rickety elevator, department policy or not. Of course, he realizes the brass are right in this instance. The decrepit lifts found in buildings of this sort are treacherous.

They're on the fifth floor at last and the door to the fire apartment is open. Dense clouds of smoke are pushing through the open door and there's the glow of flame in the distance. Anderson, on hands and knees, starts to crawl down a long narrow hallway.

Murray and Fitzmaurice are on the sixth floor and are working on the door of the apartment directly over the fire. Larry has inserted the adz end of the Halligan tool into the doorjamb. Murray, using the flat head of the axe, pounds the Halligan into the doorjamb for greater purchase. Using the length of the tool as a lever, this pair of bull-like firefighters pry until the door snaps open. They're met with a rush of smoke and heat almost beyond endurance. They hit the floor and crawl down the long hallway. They'll search the apartment, ventilate where possible and take a frightful beating in the process. Fitzie heads down the long hallway leading to the front rooms, and Murray will search the rooms adjoining the hallway. During this process, it's possible these men will contemplate the advantages of other occupations.

Roger Brennan has the nozzle, and as the line reaches the second floor, he makes a vow of perpetual sobriety. Since this is the sixth or seventh such vow he's made this year, such promises must be taken with a grain of salt. He's already tossed his cookies all over one of the landings. He has only one consolation. If all goes well, Chief McCarthy might slip in the mess and make it all worthwhile.

Gillian and Silensa have reached the roof and forced open the bulkhead door releasing a huge cloud of smoke from the building's interior. They've looked over the edge of the roof and inspected all window locations for possible trapped occupants. Since these areas are clear, they'll concentrate on a thorough inspection of the roof surface. They'll be looking for possible extension into the cockloft and bulkhead sections.

They can hear sirens of approaching apparatus; they separate in order to finish the job as rapidly as possible. There's a strong indication their presence will be required below. They'll have to hurry. The guys below could be in trouble, deep trouble.

As he reaches the fifth floor with the lieutenant, Bernie Schwartz wishes with all his heart that he might be back in the office figuring out an insurance problem. This is one hell of a situation. There's a long narrow smoke-filled hallway. Directly off this hallway are numerous rooms. At the end of the hallway are still other rooms completely involved in flame. The lieutenant will search the rooms off the hallway. Bernie will use the extinguisher in an attempt to contain conditions long enough to enable Anderson to complete his mission. As he crawls down the hallway Bernie is not unmindful of Muriel's advice. "Bernie, you're out of your mind!"

Lieutenant Anderson has just finished searching the second of three rooms directly off the hallway of the heavily involved apartment. Two down and one to go. He's looked under beds and in the closets. One must always be mindful of small children's tendency to hide from danger. He's used his helmet to smash the windows of each room in an effort to ventilate. He's closed the door of each room to limit eventual fire spread. He moves on to the third room.

The lieutenant's search of the third room has been productive. The woman's unconscious form had been near the window. He shoulders the victim and staggers towards the hallway noting, to his horror, the overhead rush of flame. The hallway is starting to light up. "Bernie, bail out! The joint is lighting up! Bail out!"

Anderson reels down the hallway and dives through the entrance leading toward the floor landings. He drops the woman and turns to look for Schwartz. He's not there and the hallway is fully involved in flame. "Bernie! Bernie! Oh, my God, Bernie!" There is no answer.

Getting as close to the fire as possible, Bernie has directed the contents of the extinguisher into the flame. He knows the effect will be negligible. He's buying time for Anderson. As soon as the lieutenant has searched the three rooms, they'll bail out.

The heat is becoming unbearable. Bernie retreats slowly down the hallway using the extinguisher and trying to give Anderson time to do his job. He hears a voice in the distance. He notes the overhead atmosphere lighting up. He drops the extinguisher and runs.

The hallway is long and the heat intense. Bernie, stumbling, smashes his head against a wall and loses his helmet. He's becoming disoriented. He rises and comes up against a closed door. Momentarily he feels they've closed the apartment door on him. He smashes against the door, finds a handle, opens the door and dives through. It takes a moment to realize he's made a mistake. This isn't the entrance to the apartment. He's locked himself in one of the apartment rooms. He's trapped. The outside hall is fully involved in flame.

He searches for a window, leans out and shouts for help. As he looks up, he spies Billy Murray. He's saved. Billy will get help. He's going to be O.K. He's going to be O.K.

If there's a rougher fire department assignment than searching the area immediately above a fire floor, it isn't known to Murray and Fitzmaurice. As they move from room to room, groping under beds and in closets for possible victims, the punishment is intense. The heat, smoke and noxious gases at this level have to be experienced to be believed. Fitzie is handling the front rooms. Billy's taking care of the rooms off the hallway.

Murray is feeling under a bed when he hears a scream. For a moment he's confused, wondering at the source of the sound. Finally he becomes aware that the screaming is below him and he looks out of the window. He's horrified. Bernie Schwartz straddles the window immediately below. Billy shouts for Fitzie. They both head for the roof. This will be a rope job.

As Fitzmaurice and Murray rush for the roof, they are joined by Lieutenant Anderson. The veteran Anderson has realized that Schwartz's only salvation lies in a rope rescue and has instinctively headed for Silensa and Gillian and the nylon rope that would be part of their equipment.

The rope is played out and Fitzmaurice snaps the end of the nylon rope to his safety harness while Gillian inserts five turns of the rope around the hook of his Atlas life belt. Murray helps Larry over the parapet for the rescue attempt.

Anderson leans over the roof and calls encouragement to Schwartz. Larry, gripping his buddy Murray's hand tightly in a good luck handshake, takes a deep breath and goes over the side of the roof.

When Larry reached Bernie, smoke and flame were pushing through the window. Understandably, Bernie was close to panic. Larry, attempting to calm him down, tried a little humor. "Have no fear, Bernie, Larry is here! Just wrap your legs around me and make believe I'm Gina Lollabrigida." That old pro Bernie Schwartz responded admirably. "Just don't rape me on the way down!"

As he swung away from the window Larry signaled the upstairs crew to start playing out rope. They're on their way down. They've got seventy feet to go before they reach bottom.

Lieutenant Anderson, leaning over the roof, is elated. "He's got him! Larry's got him! We're going to be O.K. We're going to be O.K." As Gillian and Silensa play out the rope they can feel the tremendous weight of both men. They call for Murray to lend a hand. For a thirty-second period the three men strain against the descending weight. Suddenly there's nothing . . . absolutely nothing. No strain, no weight, no tension. Just the feeling of nothing on the end of the line.

The three men stand looking at the horrified lieutenant. His face is ghastly. The man has suddenly aged twenty years in the space of a second. He attempts to mouth words but nothing comes out. Finally he speaks. "The rope. The fucking rope. It broke. The goddamned thing just snapped and they're both on the bottom of the shaft!"

The air shaft's bottom is some seventy feet below the fifth floor window.

Aftermath to a Tragedy

Reactions to the tragedy at box 1377 vary. Union officials demand an investigation. Ranking officers assigned to the upper echelon engage in evasive action. The press, digging in all directions, seems confused. The attempts of a host of reporters to saddle someone—or anyone—with responsibility adds to the general confusion.

For a time most firefighters are inclined to accept the rationale of the brass. The accident is due to tragic circumstance. The similarity to a stroke of lightning, an earthquake or an act of God exists. The ever present reasoning that the firefighter's lot is a hazardous one meets general acceptance. Besides, there are things to be done. Firefighters consider themselves to be all part of one family. There are two brothers to be buried, wives to be consoled and children to be comforted. And so for the moment, judgment on the part of the firefighter is reserved.

The privacy of grief accorded to the normal individual during a time of bereavement is startlingly absent for the firefighter slain in the performance of duty. Their interment is a rather public spectacle. To the average person it seems similar to a three-ring circus, Super Bowl Sunday, or the arrival of a celebrity. The veteran firefighter finds it rather repetitious. It's an event that's taking place all too often. Of course, it's a time for the politically motivated to be seen, to be heard and to be quoted concerning their love for the public servant. It is fully understood that these same officials will treat them in a miserly fashion at some later date concerning any demand for a living wage.

The funerals are scheduled for the same day. Bernie Schwartz will be buried from Brooklyn in the morning. The services for Larry Fitzmaurice will be held in Laurelton, Long Island in the early afternoon. Logistics concerning the movement of apparatus and personnel have been carefully worked out. Every off duty member will attend both funerals.

The essentially disparate nature of these two men will accompany them to their graves. Bernie will go as quietly as possible under the circumstances. The casket, draped with the American flag indicating his service to his country, is carried on the shoulders of six uniformed members of Engine 58 and Ladder 26 and placed on a department pumper. The grieving Muriel, her two sons, and the executive board of the Fire Department Naer Tormad Society exit from the funeral home on Avenue "O" and Coney Island Avenue and accompany Bernie to the family plot on Long Island.

The streets are lined with the row on row of off duty uniformed firefighters. Thousands of local Brooklynites jam the area. In accordance with Muriel's wishes, the grave site ceremonies will be private. Whether Muriel still considers Bernie to have been out of his mind is a matter for conjecture, something only she knows. It's more than certain his colleagues regarded him as useful.

Larry Fitzmaurice's funeral is something else. In contrast to the privacy maintained by the Schwartz family, Larry and his clan have been gregarious by nature. They love people, excitement and noise. They're a huge family, these Fitzmaurices, and very closely knit. The father, a retired firefighter, has sired ten. Each married child in turn has a large family. All of them love one another and all of them mourn Larry. They will demonstrate their loyalty to Larry and go to one another on this last day of Larry's tenure. They will see him off in style. They will make it a day to remember. In so doing, in their fashion, they will immortalize Larry.

The Church of the Resurrection in Laurelton is packed to capacity. This is where Larry served as an altar boy. His mother and his sisters find nothing incongruous in such past service. Not so with Larry's best friend, Billy Murray. Murray's brokenheartedly going over in his mind the hundreds of bizarre episodes Larry'd engaged in. He remembers the man, not the boy.

The eulogy is rather unusual. Each adult member of the Fitzmaurice family has something to say, something that reminds them of Fitz. It's rather eloquent and certainly not unusual that Larry's wife Eileen remembers him best of all. Her description of Larry's philosophy is magnificent: "Larry often told me it's a great life if you don't weaken, but it's a lot more fun if you do!"

Outside of this magnificent church thousands of uniformed firefighters lined up for a farewell salute to the flag-draped casket. Like Bernie, Larry is a combat veteran. Among the thousands present are hundreds of off duty police officers. These men wear their badges pinned to the outside of their coat jackets, and each badge is adorned with a piece of black tape indicating sympathy for the departed firefighters.

The Emerald Society Piper Band is present and those intent on hearing a dirge will be disappointed. The playing of a dirge is not part of the Fitzmaurice family philosophy. As the cortege moves slowly out, the Piper Band breaks into the stirring, lilting, breathtaking airs of "The Gary Owen." Larry is going out the way he lived. Larry is going out in style.

It's possible that many persons seeing the huge funeral procession disappearing in the distance might consider matters closed. They would be wrong. This is no ordinary family. There's more to do than leave Larry in the Veterans Cemetery in Eastern Long Island. Much more.

Within three hours the Fitzmaurice family and their friends will gather at the Volunteer Fire House that serves the Laurelton community. There they will celebrate Larry's life. They will sing, they will dance, they will remember this bruising hulk of a man in all his magnificence. The stories of his heroism, his insanities, his love of life, his love of family, love of country, love of God, but more than anything else his love for the fire department will be told and retold and then told again. And then, and only then, will the Fitzmaurices go home and weep.

Since it isn't every day that a roof rope snaps during a rescue attempt, it would be only natural that the press keep on top of the matter. They picked, they pried, they made demands and finally, almost reluctantly, a defective portion of the coping on the roof of the fire building was shown to the press. Department officials explained that coping is the material used as the uppermost portion of the roof parapet. Additionally, they informed the press that the coping normally has a smooth glazed surface. The break in the piece shown formed a knife-like edge. This *perfectly adequate* rope simply could not stand being sawed across a sharp-edged crevice while bearing the weight of two men. It was an act of God.

The Uniformed Firefighters Association made demands for an analysis of the rope. It wasn't that the organization doubted the members of the upper echelon; they simply felt impelled to protect their members in the event the rope *was* defective. Their request was denied.

It's possible that the matter might have died a natural death. After all, tragedies of this sort tend to become nine-day wonders. Fire department widows and fire department orphans are soon forgotten by the general public. There was, however, one chink in the armor of those attempting to bury this tragic affair. A man with a guilty conscience.

Three weeks have passed since her husband's death and Eileen Fitzmaurice is now truly bereaved. The excitement, the turmoil, the publicity have all subsided. At last it has finally sunk in. Larry is never coming home. This was the day she emptied her mailbox of its contents and discovered the document in all its horror—indicating culpability on the part of Larry's superiors. This was the day Eileen Fitzmaurice became aware that the rope had been declared *grossly inadequate well in advance* of this Harlem tragedy. This was the day she became aware that Larry and his friend Bernie should not have died at box 1377. Being a very determined individual, she embarked on a campaign to uncover every facet concerning this tragic incident.

Eileen engaged an attorney and called a press conference. Her attorney would have preferred springing this photostat concerning the rope's shortages in court. It would certainly have been in the best interest of Eileen Fitzmaurice and her family. Eileen, however, would have no part in this type strategy. The ropes were *still* carried on every piece of apparatus serving the New York City community. Two firemen had died as a result of the rope's inadequacies. As far as this courageous lady is concerned, they will be the last.

Reaction to this dramatic news was immediate. The press was up in arms. They smelled a cover-up and they attacked the upper echelon of the department without mercy. The Uniformed Firefighters Association demanded an impartial investigation. The brass brazened it out. The rope was O.K. It was the best available. There was no need to panic.

Reaction in the ranks was close to mutinous. For years the officers and members of this department, serving literally in the front lines, had forged ahead insofar as the protection of life and property was concerned. This was something else. If the rope was defective, what next? Could they trust a mask? An extinguisher? A length of hose? *Does anybody care?*

Realizing the enormity of the situation, the Mayor of this huge city finally stepped in and appointed what was described as an impartial fact-finding commission. Despite the evidence clearly indicating the rope's deficiency, the inquiry dragged on. It dragged on for a length of time sufficient to enable two of the highest ranking officials in the department to retire on magnificent lifetime pensions.

Finally, the commission's report was released. The rope was declared grossly inadequate. It would be removed from all apparatus and replaced by a substitute capable of performing the functions required.

Naturally there had to be a zinger. It just wouldn't be natural for an investigative committee of this type to fold its tent and depart without putting the onus on a completely blameless victim. Carried away by their own importance, they extended their investigation into operations at box 1377 itself.

The fact that there wasn't a member of the fire department on the committee failed to stop these people from waxing pontifical on matters beyond their fields of expertise. In view of the efforts of the upper echelon to cover their tracks in the matter of the rope, failure to include superior officers of the department met with general approval. Such approval ended when this committee attempted to stick the harpoon into one of the department's own. The firefighters were up in arms.

Lieutenant Frank Anderson was the victim selected for pillorying. After all, some effort had to be made to get the city off the hook. Despite complete ignorance concerning operations at large fires, these people rendered judgment. It was their opinion that Schwartz should not have been sent down the hallway in an attempt to buy time for Anderson. The rescue, in their opinion, could have proceeded without Schwartz's presence. Their expertise on rescue procedures was not further explained. Furthermore, they had the audacity to indicate Anderson had used poor judgment in sending Fitzie over the side so soon. They rationalized that an engine company would have been in position in a matter of minutes. None of them indicated whether or not they've ever sat on the windowsill of a heavily involved room awaiting the arrival of help.

Definitive action on this phase of the operation was never pursued by city officials. Perhaps the implied threat of a general walkout by members in the event of any such action might have had some effect.

Nevertheless, a copy of this report had been sent to Lieutenant Anderson. He filed it away with Jenny's letter. That now aged Dear John epistle received on yet another battlefield, indicating a teenaged girl's heartlessness was fitting companion for the committee's report. Frank loves the fire department and he loves Jenny. He's used to being screwed by those he loves. It's all part of the game.

Epilogue

The feelings of outrage associated with the tragedy at box 1377 affected the average member of the department rather like a nine-day wonder. The men were laid low for a while. That members of the upper echelon would adopt such a cavalier attitude regarding the personal safety of the men on the firefront was, of course, a disturbing revelation. Then, like the battered pugilist rising to one knee, pulling himself up the ropes to renew the battle, so the firefighter personally unaquainted with Schwartz and Fitzmaurice shook off the matter and resumed their protection of the city. This, of course, was for the best. Life must go on.

For members of the Fire Factory it was something else again. The men who worked on a day-to-day basis with this indomitable pair found recovery difficult. Reaction varied from individual to individual.

Frank Anderson retired. The possibility of reporting for duty and becoming involved in a similar incident was simply too much. The cessation of activities associated with a twenty-seven year career would take its toll. For this man civilian life had been an avocation. The fire department was everything. It had been his very reason for existence. Life would become a continuous visit to a local bar, a constant attempt to drown sorrow, an unceasing effort to remove the horror of two bodies plunging endlessly, turning over and over on the way to the bottom of that shaft.

The man would put on weight, lose muscle tone and develop the habit of staring endlessly hour after hour at the wall in front of his bar stool. Attempts by members of the Fire Factory to interest Frank in a variety of company activities would fail. For all practical purposes, the man's retirement from the human race would be total and complete.

Pudgy Dunn's reaction would be predictable. The number 62 would be retired from the fire department football roster, never to be worn again. During a two-week period of deep mourning, Pudgy would mumble over and over again "Them bastards and their dollar fucking ninety-eight cent rope."

Pudgy would never forget these two, but by his very nature his actions would vary from the severe melancholia destroying Frank Anderson. He would be out of City Island within six weeks. His haunting of union officials and other persons with even a smidgen of influence would bear fruit. While he didn't make it back to Harlem, Pudgy did wind up with a ghetto assignment. Transferred to Ladder 108 in Brooklyn's Williamsburgh section, he wasn't there a week before he participated in a rescue sufficiently spectacular to warrant presentation of the department's most prestigious award. The James Gordon Bennett Medal. For probably the first time in department history, the designated recipient of this award raised an uproar regarding its presentation. Pudgy considered Fitzmaurice as the logical recipient. He refused to consider the department's policy against posthumous awards and finally turned the medal over to Larry's oldest son. His rationale was simple: "Them shitheads downtown. What do they know about fucking anything?"

Oscar Ratner found it necessary to travel to Brooklyn to visit Muriel Schwartz. Haunted by the fact that he owed twenty dollars to Bernie, Oscar tearfully pleaded with Muriel to accept the money as a genuine token of affection for her husband. The lovely Muriel accepted the twenty and added it to the thousand dollars she'd anonymously donated to the fund raised for the widow and orphans of Larry Fitzmaurice.

John Silensa never cooked another firehouse meal. His heart simply wasn't in it. His explanation was simple: "I keep seeing the two of them sitting at the table. It's just too much!"

Jim Gillian expressed his grief by going on a two-week bender. During the period, he collected four traffic tickets and culminated his binge by totalling his car. His explanation that he was growing tired of the heap failed to mollify his outraged wife.

It's understandable that the man most affected by this heartbreaking incident would be Larry's closest friend, Billy Murray. One of the Bookends had been destroyed physically, and for a while, it seemed the other might go down the tube emotionally. Billy stopped studying. He put the books away and for hours at a time he closeted himself in his room at home refusing to speak to anyone. His feelings for *the job* changed drastically. Only his family obligations and the need for a paycheck kept him on the department roster. Shortly, he performed an act almost without precedent among ghetto firefighters. Using his skills obtained from training at the United States Merchant Marine Academy, he took and passed an examination for promotion to the rank of Marine Engineer. He finds his assignment to a Staten Island fireboat boring but it does have its compensations. The possibility of seeing a friend plunging down another shaft is rather unlikely.

If one were to seek trouble with Harry Murray, a mere comparison of the man with his mortal enemy, Pudgy Dunn would do the trick. Nevertheless, they're as similar as two peas in a pod. Like Pudgy, Bill's dad went into deep mourning for a reasonable period, and again like Pudgy, he pulled out with the realization that life must continue. Being disappointed at his own failure to attain higher rank, this Harlem veteran will keep pushing and prodding, making a great pest of himself in the process, until such time as his son reluctantly picks up his study material in self-defense.

Willie Burrell's reactions were totally unpredictable. This quiet, introspective man kept to himself for all of two months and spoke only when necessary. His karate partner's promotion and transfer elicited no comment. For most of his life in the firehouse he sat in a chair adjacent to his locker and stared at the wall. On a particularly quiet afternoon, right after the P.M. roll call, he suddenly issued a blood curdling scream and smashed his right fist into his locker door, totally destroying the device. Turning slowly to the seven or eight amazed firefighters who were changing their clothes, he smilingly apologized. "Sorry, guys! Just something I had to get out of my system!"

Within one month after the tragic deaths of Fitzmaurice and Schwartz, Battalion Chief McCarthy was promoted to the rank of Deputy Chief of Department. In a matter of six months he had been pushed up to the rank of Deputy Assistant Chief of Department, and then Assistant Chief of Department.

The rank of Chief of Department is vacant for the moment. It won't be vacant for long. It's been a civil service rank for years. But of late the spot has been filled by appointment.

Chief McCarthy's the prime favorite for the position. He has all the qualifications. He's handsome, makes a fine appearance in uniform, and at any public function has a host of Harlem stories to tell. He's seriously contemplating writing a book concerning his experiences.

On the anniversary of the deaths of these two members of the Fire Factory, appropriate ceremonies were held at the firehouse. A plaque commemorating the heroism and dedication of these stalwarts was installed on the wall to keep company with the two already in place. The numerous officials presiding over the ceremonies praised the dedication, fortitude and spirit of men who devoted their lives to the citizenry of New York City. Some two weeks later the same officials attended the testimonial dinner honoring the civic accomplishments of the two ranking officers of the upper echelon forced into retirement by the rope rescue scandal. Seemingly they found nothing incongruous in their presence at both functions. As usual, it was Pudgy who best phrased the feelings of the average firefighter: "A politician is a politician is a fucking politician!"

And so it ends. Or maybe it just begins. Harlem is still with us along with the rest of the city's ghettos. Sirens still scream, apparatus still roar through the streets and buildings still burn in great profusion. This tragedy does, however, have one compensation. Each apparatus now has an adequate rope—rather like a monument to Larry and to Bernie. While it's a small consolation, at least it's consolation that might save a life.